Bridezilla  vs Zombies

Katie Fraser

Also by Katie Fraser

The Realm of the Lilies Series
Through the Fig Tree
Water Off a Dragon's Back

The Shadows of Miss Pring

Magic Mama – Headaches and Heartburn

This book is a first edition.

First published November 2022
Copyright © 2022 K E Fraser
Cover Art © 2022 Belinda Crawford
All rights reserved.
Ebook ISBN 13: 978-0-6480590-5-9

This book is for Anne and David,
who always asked how my writing was going,
even after the many times I said it wasn't going at all.

Enjoy!

February 14, 3:01 p.m.
Get me to the church on time

It was official, I was late for my own wedding.

Sure, the bride doesn't traditionally walk down the aisle right on time, but that's usually to allow late guests to take their seats, not because they are having issues removing a Louboutin spiked heel from the eye socket of an undead corpse. Or maybe it was just a dead corpse by that time, it was unmoving on the ground, that heel seemed to do some damage.

Finally, with a wet schlunk, the heel came free. Shrugging, I grabbed a handful of tulle from near the hemline of my trashed dress and wiped the blood, brains and vitreous humour from the heel. I successfully fought the urge to scour between the rhinestones, this was not the time, and pulled the shoe back onto my foot.

I really had to find another weapon or maybe another pair of shoes. I eyed the corpse in front of me. It was a female. She had been dressed for farm work when struck undead and wore thick jeans, a long-sleeved shirt and sturdy work boots. Her boots were still on her feet.

I eyed them dubiously. They looked like they would fit me.

I shuddered at the thought of wearing a dead woman's shoes, but dammit, even if they wouldn't get me to the church on time, they might help me get there alive.

And, let's face it, I had done worse things already on the road to my nuptials and would probably do worse still.

I took the shoes.

July, the year before last
Bonding over Soup

"He's looking at you again," Leila hip-checked me as she teased.

"Oh God, not Grady again?" I asked, "It doesn't seem to matter how many times I tell the guy I'm looking for someone who still has at least half his teeth, he still tries to flirt every week."

Leila giggled. "No, not Grady. He's already finished eating and is checking out the insides of his eyelids over in the corner."

She pointed to him, leaning back in a recliner on the far side of the room.

Poor old guy, the few hours of shut eye he caught in the soup kitchen whenever he dropped by were probably the only snatches he caught on a soft surface.

"I was talking about him."

Leila used her soup ladle to subtly point to the guy who was moving around the tables, clearing bowls, wiping spills and chatting with the homeless people who were receptive.

"What was his name? Joseph?" I asked Leila.

"Yeah, I think so."

I watched the guy for another minute. He wiped the table with long, easy movements, sweeping the crumbs into an empty bowl. His pants looked as though they had been pressed, but he'd been in them all day, as did his long-sleeved shirt. When I'd caught glimpses of him before, he'd been in jeans and a t-shirt. I wondered if he had been stuck at the office until it was time for him to come to the soup kitchen tonight.

"How many times do you think we've seen him now?

Three? Four?" I asked.

"I don't know." Leila smiled and raised her eyebrow at me. "*I* haven't been counting."

I rolled my eyes. Of course, Leila hadn't noticed the new cute guy. She was happily bubbling over Nate, the guy who would be her husband in 3 months, fourteen days and twenty-one hours. Leila might not be counting how many times we had seen Joseph, but she was definitely counting down to her wedding. And had put a countdown on my phone home screen; she thought it was important for me to keep track, too, since I was her maid of honour.

Leila is my oldest and dearest friend. I hope that one day, she'll return the favour and be my matron of honour when I get married.

Speaking of getting married, I wondered whether Mr Rumpled was on the market.

Joseph looked up as if he sensed my scrutiny and caught me staring at him. I fought the urge to immediately look away and made eye contact with him instead. The smile on my face when our eyes met was mirrored with his own.

Unfortunately, he was called over by the volunteer manager just as he looked about to move towards us at the serving bench. He gave me a small wave as he moved away in the opposite direction.

"Oh, you look disappointed," Leila said. "Have I just witnessed love at first sight being thwarted?"

I sighed. "I don't know. Maybe. But it wasn't first sight anyway. We've seen him before, remember?"

I finished scraping the last of the soup from my pot into two waiting bowls and moved towards the kitchen with my dishes.

"I'll be back in a minute," I told Leila as I walked away.

The smirk on her face said she knew exactly what I was hoping to find while in the kitchen, and it wasn't a fresh pot of potato and bacon soup.

Vanessa, the volunteer manager, was still talking to Joseph when I walked around them to put my pot in the sink.

They were poring over the roster posted on the kitchen wall, talking quietly but intensely, studying the staff allocations. Vanessa's forehead held the little furrow that generally graced it when she was worried.

"Is something wrong?" I asked her when I had handed my pot off to one of the kitchen team.

"Hmm, oh! Hi, Lucy." She turned her lips upward into an expression that didn't quite manage to be a smile. "No, nothing is *wrong*. We're just trying to solve a little volunteer staffing problem. You know how stretched we've been lately. Cold and flu season can be a real problem sometimes."

"And you know, *Lucy*." He said my name like he was relishing that he finally knew what to call me. "Where a lot of people would soldier on through illness for their day job, they don't necessarily feel the need to press on for their volunteer work. Even though the homeless don't just stop coming because our volunteers are sick."

"Sad but true," I said.

Some nights, I just wanted to sit on my couch and forget about serving bowls of soup or washing a hundred or so bowls and spoons. Sometimes, it was only my friendship with Leila that got me out of the house and into the soup kitchen, and I was pretty sure the same could be said for her too.

"So, what particular shortfall are you trying to fill tonight?" I asked.

Vanessa sighed. "Nothing you can help with, I'm afraid. We're short a kitchen hand tomorrow night. You've got down that you can't help on Thursday nights."

"I'm already on shift," Joseph said. "So, I'm no good to her either."

I looked at Joseph again. Leila and I had assumed he was new to the volunteer team, but maybe he just didn't normally come in on our regular night in the soup kitchen.

"Well, as it happens, my Thursday commitment has

5

been cancelled this week, so I can come in and help out."

The corners of Vanessa's lips pitched upward into what was definitely a smile this time.

"Could you? That would be amazing."

"Sure. What shift is it?"

I hoped it wasn't sink duty.

All the volunteers rolled through the different work positions. That night, Leila and I were serving, Joseph was on dishes and two other people were on sink duty: the joyous fun of plunging your hands into hot, soapy water for hours on end.

"The one spot left to be filled is sink duty," Joseph said. "But I'll do you a favour. I'm on dishes again tomorrow, but I don't really like doing the same job two nights in a row. I'll do the sink if you do the dishes."

He winked and smiled at me, showing a mouthful of almost perfect teeth. I say almost perfect because my attention was drawn to one incisor that hooked slightly to the side, just covering its neighbour.

"Well, that won me over. I just got a fresh manicure." I waved my unpainted fingernails in their direction to show I was joking.

He laughed.

"Perfect."

"Thank you so much," Vanessa said. "You are a life saver, Luce."

"No problem at all." I smiled and turned to Joseph. "I guess I'll see you tomorrow night."

The next day
So much soup

By the second hour of my first ever Thursday night at the soup kitchen, I regretted accepting Joe's offer to let me take the dishes.

Apparently, something happened on Thursday nights that made it one of the busiest nights of the week.

"Is it just me, or did the homeless population double overnight?"

I plunked yet another load of bowls down on the sink next to Joseph's elbow.

He groaned. "I would laugh, but I need to save my energy for cleaning these bowls and getting them out again for the next round."

Vanessa hovered over the industrial cooktop. The steam from the third round of defrosting soups caused her hair to frizz out of its bun.

"Is it usually this busy on a Thursday?" I asked, taking a moment to lean against the bench.

"I don't know. Thursday isn't usually my day either."

A disembodied head appeared around the dining room door and shouted.

"We're going to run out of bowls again soon."

I whimpered as I pushed myself upright. My Fitbit gave a little buzz on my wrist as it told me I had reached 13,000 steps, double my usual daily goal, which I barely made most days. My feet screamed that they wished I had worn my running shoes and super expensive jogging socks. Why was I treating my poor feet with such disrespect?

Another person on sink duty had dried the most recent batch of bowls and put them on the bench. I gave myself a little pep talk, picked up the clean bowls and returned to the dining room.

Another hour later, all the soup was gone, all the homeless bellies were full, and Joseph was washing his last sink of dishes.

I was sitting on an upturned milk crate, ignoring the pain the plastic mesh was inflicting on my behind. At least when I was sitting, I couldn't feel the pain in my feet.

"My God, that was intense," I said.

Even the normally unflappable Vanessa was ragged around the edges. She walked up and looked like she was about to slump to the floor before realising it was coated with dish suds. I reached behind me and hooked a few fingers through another milk crate. The plastic rattled and scraped as I pulled the crate around for her to sit on. She sagged down gratefully.

"I think it's the cold snap," she said. "I think every single man, woman and child we serve came in here tonight. I don't think that has ever happened in the eight years I've been the manager here."

"I counted eleven soup pots through the sink tonight."

Eleven! The next biggest night I could remember had reached seven pots. Though I didn't have the energy to bring that point up in conversation, I was talked out.

As Joseph had been so smoothly demonstrating the night before, part of dishes duty was also trying to engage with the homeless people who used the service. Even if it was just to get them to nod when you ask them if they had a nice day. These people had learnt to be so protective of themselves that it was sometimes hard to even get that.

I was exhausted from running back and forth all night and trying to show people that we were operating a safe place for them find sustenance and shelter.

"Nearly done," Joseph said.

Despite his earlier comment about needing to preserve his energy, he still seemed to have a bit of cheer in him.

I didn't know whether to be impressed or disgusted.

Joseph was a morning person bouncing like a pinball around us, the people who hadn't caffeinated.

"Well, I've done the last dishes run anyway," I said. "If a single spoon is left out in that dining room, I don't know where it is hiding."

"Yep, we are clear out there," Vanessa said, "I just finished running the mop over the floors. I will tear off the little toes of anyone who sets a dirty sneaker."

"Aaand, that's the sign that it's time for Vanessa to go home."

The water gurgling out of the sink punctuated Joseph's words as he put the last bowl on the draining rack.

The dish drier had left after Joseph had told him the last few dishes could air-dry, so it was just the three of us left in the kitchen.

"You two are done." Vanessa gave us a wan smile. "I just need to write my report, and then I'll lock up and head home. Thank you both for your help tonight."

"You're welcome," I said.

"See you next week," Joseph said.

We headed towards the back door together.

"I feel like I should apologise for dragging you in here tonight," Joseph said as we reached the exit.

"Well, you didn't know it was going to be so crazy, so I don't think you need to," I said.

He opened the door for me, and the fresh, cold air buffeted my face. I shivered.

"Well, maybe I don't need to apologise, but I could take you for a thank you coffee?" He suggested.

"No coffee after midday for me," I said.

He looked a little crestfallen, "I would suggest ice cream, but it's probably too cold..."

"It's never too cold for ice cream," I said, "but maybe I would prefer a hot chocolate?"

"Hot chocolate, we can do," he smiled. He pointed to the few cars in the back car park. "Did you drive tonight?"

"No, I caught the bus this morning and came straight

from work."

"That's easy then. Let me take you to a coffee shop, and then I can give you a ride home."

A moment of worry crossed my mind as I remembered all the warnings about accepting rides from strangers.

As if sensing where my thoughts had gone, Joseph said, "I have my Police Clearance certification in the car if you want to take a look. I promise I'm not a serial killer."

I smiled. Of course, he wasn't a serial killer; he volunteered in a soup kitchen, for heaven's sake.

"Well, they didn't find any evidence of you being a serial killer the last time they did your police check." I made sure he could see my smile as I spoke.

"Ah yes, the evidence, they'll never find that, mwah-ha-hah!"

Yep, he actually gave a fake maniacal laugh.

"Right. I'm going to leave that one alone. Don't you want to know where I live before you offer me a ride home? I could be all the way on the opposite side of town."

"Lucy, the opposite side of anywhere in this town is a maximum of a forty-five-minute drive. I would rather spend two hours driving you somewhere and two hours driving home alone than leave you to catch the bus in this chill."

His words sent a little thrill of warmth up my arms to my neck. How could a girl turn down an offer like that?

"Okay. Thank you." I said. "But I'm paying for the coffee."

"You can try."

First date
Coffee or chocolate?

Is it still considered a date if someone is just buying you a hot chocolate when you are absolutely exhausted and your feet hurt from running around wildly for 4 hours straight?

I don't care. I'm calling it a date.

"I can't believe we haven't crossed each other's paths before now," Joseph said. "How long did you say you'd been volunteering in the soup kitchen?"

He led the way, weaving between chairs to a small table in the back corner of the café. We each carried a mug of chocolate flanked by puffy, powdered marshmallows.

"A little less than three years. We…er, my friend Leila and I, always volunteer on Wednesday nights." I was babbling. I needed to stop babbling. Lord, I was tired. "You?"

"About two. I moved to town to be with my parents." He looked momentarily mortified. "Not that I needed to be with my parents. I am an adult and have my own place, but they moved to Sky Valley about five years ago, and when I got my degree, I decided to come here too. We're a close family."

He finished his own round of verbal diarrhea with a smile, kicking up the corner of his mouth to show off that cute little crooked tooth.

"That's adorable." I covered my mouth. I couldn't believe I'd said that out loud. "I mean, it's so lovely that you could move to be close again. What do you do?"

"I'm a financial advisor, you?"

"Cool! I'm in social media management, so we both kind of help people improve their net worth. You help people directly by telling them where to invest their money. And I help people and businesses plan their social media campaigns to increase their income."

He chuckled. "I guess we do."

My gaze kept being pulled to his eyes. They were a magnetic steel grey, with little crinkles that deepened whenever he laughed or smiled. I found myself acting goofy in an attempt to get him to laugh just so I could see those crinkles.

Our comfortable chatter was interrupted by the buzzing of my mobile. I would have ignored it, but the sound of Cher belting out 'Love Hurts' indicated that my mother was on the other end of the line.

I groaned. "I'm sorry, do you mind if I take this? It's my Mum."

"Go right ahead. I'll just check my email." He pulled out his own phone and tapped his finger on the screen.

I swiped the answer icon up, braced myself and put the phone to my ear.

"Hi, Mum. What's up?"

"Lucy, honey. I was worried when you didn't show up to dinner tonight. Is everything okay?"

I quickly glanced at Joseph, hoping he was absorbed in his emails, and chose my words carefully.

"I called Dad earlier today and explained. Didn't he tell you?"

"Well, he said something about that homeless place, but you don't do that on Thursday because we have family dinner. Remember, you said you'd make family dinner? I hope this isn't going to become a regular thing. You know how I feel..."

"Yes, Mum." I finally found a place to interrupt. "I know how you feel. I just needed to help out tonight, that's all."

I stared determinedly at the napkin I was concertina folding and hoped that I had only imagined Joseph sitting a little more upright in his chair at my last comment.

"Well, I should hope so. You know how important it is to

me that we get together every week, you and your brother..."

"Yes, Mum, I know. We're your pride and joy." I kept talking before Mum's sniff at being interrupted could turn into a lecture. "I'm sorry, Mum, I have to go. I'm just having a coffee with a friend after our shift..."

"A coffee?! Honey, caffeine after midday? Your complexion!"

"Figure of speech, Mum. I'm having hot chocolate, but I am out with a friend, and it's very rude of me to be on my phone. I made an exception because I knew it was you calling, but...."

"Of course! You have to go."

My mother was very proper when it came to phone etiquette. And etiquette and manners in general.

"Call me tomorrow evening, will you dear? Explain it all to me then."

"Yes, Mum. Love you."

"Love you too." She blew two air kisses down the line and hung up.

I stared at my phone for a moment before stuffing it back in my pocket and being caught in the pull of his eyes again.

I sighed. "Parents. Can't live with them, wouldn't be alive without them."

He chuckled.

He reached across the table for my hand, a little buzz ran up my fingers as he pulled them into his palm. He turned my hand over and drew circles in my palm with his index finger, sending proper goosebumps up my arm.

"So," He turned a cheeky grin towards me. "I thought you said your plans for tonight had been cancelled?"

The warmth that rose in my cheeks was from more than the sizzle his touch was giving me.

"Did I? I must have misspoken. I meant I would cancel my plans for tonight. Or maybe you misheard. That kitchen can get quite noisy."

"I don't believe you."

13

I tried to pull my hand away in a show of pique, but his fingers tightened in reflex, and he held it close.

"See," he said, "I think you just wanted a reason to see me again."

I cocked my head at him. "Well, you must think highly of yourself."

My heart was pounding.

"And you know what?" he asked, still holding my hand.

I shook my head and shrugged.

"I'm glad you did because I really wanted to see you again too."

This is it, I told myself. I think he's the one. I wonder if he feels the same.

We'd lingered over our hot chocolates until the waitress had to shoo us out so she could close, and it was nearly 11 p.m. when Joseph pulled his car into the drive of my little unit.

"This is home, huh?" He asked casually.

The way he said it, it was like he was asking if it could be his home too. A little frisson of excitement filled me at the thought, but wariness cautioned me not to get too excited so quickly.

"I'll walk you to your door."

It was a whole 4 metres from the front of the car.

"Oh, you don't have to..."

But he was already out.

He'd left the engine running and the keys in the ignition, which I took as a sign he wasn't expecting to be invited in.

I fumbled for my keys in my handbag before getting out of the car. The cool, crisp air buffeted my face as I opened the door and stepped out into the night.

He held out his hand for mine at the corner of the bonnet, then enveloped my cold fingers within his warm ones.

We walked the few steps to my front door together, our double shadows cast by the car's headlights preceding us.

14

We turned to face each other in the sheltered entrance.

"Lucy, I..."

"Joseph, it..."

We both laughed.

"You first," I said.

"Okay. I had a really nice time with you tonight."

I tried to lighten the moment. "I know. I must be the best dish collector you've ever worked with."

He laughed. "Well, that's true, but the bit after was good too."

The little crooked tooth in the corner of his mouth appeared.

"I thought so too."

We'd already exchanged phone numbers, so there wasn't really anything else to say.

We stood in silence for a moment, staring weirdly at each other.

"Um." I said. "Thanks for giving me a ride home."

"Any time," he said. "Absolutely any time."

Before leaving, he kissed me.

The second date

Not the piecework

"So, what else do you like to do in your spare time?" Joseph asked me over his glass of wine.

"Aside from volunteering at the soup kitchen?" I asked. "Well, I am quite keen on a good Netflix binge session, and I'm also part of a group who stitch up quilts."

"Oh, like the ones donated to the shelter?"

His eyes glittered in the dim light of the restaurant, competing with the glimmer from the small diamond stud in his left ear.

I smiled. "Exactly like those ones. I don't have the patience for all the piecework, but I love finishing them. Stitching the layers together and binding the edges. People think I'm crazy because I bind the work by hand, but I find it too hard with a machine. Quilts are really big and hard to handle sometimes."

His eyes lost their focus a little, and his hand stopped tapping on the table. I'd lost him.

"Well...I just like being able to put the finishing touches on things."

"No, I get that. It was just...you like stitching by hand? My Mum used to make quilts before my folks moved here, and I'd watch her finish off her quilts. It would take hours to do that sort of work on a machine. It must take you days."

I shrugged. "It's what I like to do. I usually do it when I'm watching TV, then I don't feel so bad about sitting on my butt."

He nodded his head a few times. "That's really cool."

I smiled. "Thanks. So, what do you do for fun?"

"Pretty much the same as you," he said. "Only without

the quilting part. I watch Netflix. I like walking, sometimes I'll get together with some buddies on the weekend, and we'll play basketball or cricket. I'm largely a homebody, though."

I smiled. "Me too."

We were interrupted as a waitress brought our meals and topped up our wine glasses.

As a second date, it was looking good.

November, the year before last
Wedding guests

Leila and her new husband were posing in a rose garden. She glowed in her champagne-coloured dress and gazed blissfully into Nate's eyes.

"Have you ever seen a more adorable bride and groom?" I asked.

The limo driver, who had stepped out to stretch his legs while this round of photos was being taken, looked at me sideways.

"Oh, no, definitely not." His tone didn't quite have the ring of truth to it.

I laughed. "Alright, how long have you been driving limos for weddings?"

He smiled. "Two and half years. Roughly a hundred and twenty weekends, with most weekends having two weddings. I must have driven for at least two hundred brides, but your friends are definitely the most adorable."

"Oh, Gerald, you're funny."

"Honey, are you picking on the limo driver?" Joe's voice carried as he walked towards the two of us.

In the 3 months and 13 days since we'd started seeing each other, Joe and I had become a solid couple. We'd grown so close that Leila had asked him if he wanted to join the bridal party in the limo as we schlepped about between the ceremony and reception on her wedding day, even though he wasn't a groomsman.

"I am not picking on Gerald. He was being untruthful to me."

"Uh-oh, that sounds dangerous. Quick, change the subject," Joseph joked.

I smiled and complied. "Did you know that Gerald is in the last year of his finance degree? He's hoping to become a financial advisor."

Joseph looked at me through narrowed eyelids, but the corner of his mouth quirked up slightly. "Is he?"

"Why yes, he is. I thought maybe you could give him some career advice."

Joseph shook his head at me slowly. "You are hopeless."

He caught me around the waist and pulled me in for a quick kiss before pulling me around and tucking me into his side.

He started talking to Gerald about career options and finally pulled out one of his business cards.

"Here, my email address is on that. If you send me through your academic transcript, I'll see if I can help you out."

"Thank you so much. I will definitely do that."

A warmth filled my chest. This was why I was falling in love with the guy. He was so kind and generous.

A shout from the garden drew my attention.

"Lucy? Lucy, will you come and help me?"

My bride was calling.

I made my way across the grass, balancing my weight more towards the balls of my feet so my heels wouldn't sink into the soft soil beneath the turf.

"What do you need, Mrs Bride?"

Leila giggled and smiled at me. "Can you help with my train? I had trouble holding it up on my own when we were getting over here, and Nate had to go to the bathroom."

"Of course."

I hefted the weight of the train, making sure I held it high enough that the hem wouldn't collect mud but not so high that I'd expose my friend.

"You and Joe seem pretty cosy." Leila gave me a little smile.

"Yes, we are."

I was comfortable with him. He freed me.

19

"So, will I be watching you making kissy faces at him on your wedding day?"

I smiled a little, secret smile.

"I think there is a strong possibility."

February 14, last year
Corks and questions

"Joseph! Where are you taking me!"

I giggled as I spoke, unable to hold onto my mock-temper.

"We're almost there, just a little bit...oh, watch your step there!"

My hiking boot went down awkwardly on a tree root.

He'd been leading me blindfolded along the hiking trail for almost 10 minutes. Blindfolds and rarely walked hiking trails aren't an ideal combination. Fortunately, I could peek out the bottom of my blindfold and at least keep an eye on my footing. I couldn't keep my bare legs away from the spiky bushes that grew along the edge of the path in places, but I considered not spraining an ankle to be a win.

I felt an immediate warmth on my legs as we moved from the shaded path into the open and the mid-afternoon sun hit my bare skin.

"Okay, just over here—" Joseph said, "—is a table with a bench. Slide in here."

I did so clumsily and bumped my thigh on the edge of the table. I bit back a cry of pain; he was so adorable, and I didn't want him to feel bad.

"Alright, sit right here for a minute. I just need to get a couple of things ready."

The bench was in the sun, and the warmth in the timber permeated my shorts to my hamstrings. The sun was not as fierce on my skin as it had been, though, and I thought the bench must be in dappled shade.

Bushland birds trilled, and the laugh of a Kookaburra echoed through the national park. The air was fresh and dry and marked with the light scent of eucalyptus leaves underfoot.

A light wave of air passed over me, and I felt a tickle of fabric graze my thigh. A tablecloth? I heard the clinking of plasticware, followed by thunks on the table and clicks of containers being popped.

Finally, I heard his booted feet move around the table towards me, and I felt him stand behind me.

"Alright, now we can take this off."

He undid the tie on the blindfold and dropped it from my eyes.

"Happy Valentine's Day, Lucy."

A white tablecloth dotted with tiny red hearts had been spread across the table. A board with hard and soft cheese, little pickled onions, sliced pear and crackers was set on the table. Behind was a bottle of sparkling wine and a couple of plastic flutes.

"Oh, look at this! How lovely, thank you."

I turned to kiss him in thanks. His grin sparkled, and his little wonky tooth glinted.

"You're welcome. But you haven't even seen the best bit yet."

He moved to the end of the bench next to me, so I didn't have to twist around completely to see him.

"Lucy, I'm sure you expected me to do this sometime soon. We've been pretty much inseparable for the last six months and being with you practically guarantees an awesome time."

He reached into his pocket and pulled something out before dropping to one knee in front of me.

"I just wanted to show you this."

He popped the little red velvet box open to reveal a ring, a stunning blue-green stone in the middle, flanked by two rectangular diamonds.

"And ask if you would like to, I dunno, get hitched?"

"Get hitched?" I mock shouted and gently punched him in the bicep.

He laughed. "Well?"

"'I dunno, get hitched!' You are hopeless, Joe!" I laughed back.

I gestured for him to bring the box closer so I could pretend to consider my answer based on whether or not I approved of the ring.

I approved very much, but honestly, he called that a proposal!

"Well." I heaved a breath and sighed. "I suppose you went to all that effort with the wine and the cheese. It would be a shame if it was all wasted. I dunno, I guess I'd better say yes."

February 15, last year
Simple plans

"Oh my gosh, I'm so excited for you!" Leila gushed, "I knew he would propose this weekend. I knew it!"

"Thanks for giving me the heads up," I said, laughing over my mimosa.

She grabbed a cracker and dunked it in the homemade French onion dip I'd set out on the back patio table.

It was an impromptu celebration with just the four of us. A bottle of local sparkling wine shared between Leila, Nate, Joe and me.

"You should have a Star Wars wedding!" Nate said.

"Honey, very few women on this planet would agree to a Star Wars wedding. I don't think Lucy is one of them."

I laughed. "Definitely not."

"I'm probably not the kind of man to propose a Star Wars wedding either," Joe said.

We all laughed.

"What sort of wedding do you want?" Nate asked.

"Well, I'm a bloke, so to be honest, I could get married barefoot on a pile of red-hot coals or that fancy chapel the royals get married in. As long as Lucy is there and happy, I will be too."

"A destination wedding to Westminster Abbey?" Leila's eyes lit up.

"Hot coals? Um, no," I said.

"Alright, alright," Joe said. "I wouldn't mind a small outdoor ceremony in a nice garden, though. There's that one down the south end of town with the waterfall? With a celebrant who actually knows us rather than a priest we've met three times before. That would be nice."

A hush fell across the group as we all imagined that.

"Maybe in mid-Spring. I know the place. It would be absolutely lovely down there then. We could have marquees on the grassed area and have the reception there too."

I thought about him in a nice suit, and me, in a simple dress, no tulle or taffeta, smooth lines and thick satin.

It was all we needed, really. Just me and him.

"I could get a licence and be your celebrant," Nate suggested.

Joseph smiled. "That would be good, I think. What do you reckon, Lucy?"

I filled out the tableau.

Nate as the celebrant, centred in front of the waterfall. Leila at my side, Joseph's brothers with him. Just our family and closest friends.

"Sounds perfect to me."

February 14, 8:00 a.m.
Toasts

Nora, my maid of honour, poured Champagne into five flutes and offered a toast.

"To a perfect day, for a perfect bride! To Lucy!"

My other bridesmaids repeated the toast, and I took a sip of the Champagne.

Yes, real Champagne, not sparkling chardonnay. We were starting the day the way it was going to end—in style.

"Oh, that's amazing," Bridget said.

"Isn't it good?" I asked, "Is it the first time you've ever had real Champagne?"

"Yeah, I think so."

Her voice was a little flat, but I was too excited to care, it was my day, and no-one else mattered.

I mentally checked off the details.

The church had been decorated the night before, and the chill air in the church overnight would have kept my white roses in pristine condition. They say the best way to keep your flowers fresh for longer is to keep them in the fridge overnight, and the only thing I remembered about my aunt's wedding was that the place got cold.

Joseph would arrive at the church a couple of hours before the service to have photos taken and go over his list of last-minute checks. Just because he was the groom didn't mean he wouldn't have to do anything.

His mother was lined up to check on the caterers and make sure nothing bad had happened in the marquees overnight. I had spent the previous morning checking every single piece of cutlery at each setting, making sure they were clean.

I also set out all the place cards and the carefully

packaged bonbonniere. I wrote out all of the place cards. It had taken me almost a month to master the calligraphy. When the time came, I still had to redo about 40 of the 250 place cards, but the silver ink on the teal card was perfect.

The bonbonnieres were little teal boxes filled with custom-made rock candy and tied with a silver ribbon. The inside of the candy had hearts and our names, with teal stripes on the outside.

I had been prepared to make up all the boxes and dish out all the candy on my own, but my bridesmaids had insisted on helping me. We had done it a month ago, and they had taken a lot of coaching, but after only ruining four or five each, they got the job done.

Once or twice, I had heard one of them calling me a bridezilla. Of course, I have heard the term before, and if it means that you are absolutely certain that you want every moment of your big day to be as perfect as you have imagined since you were four, then yes, you could call me a bridezilla.

I would happily accept the name.

March 1, last year

And the best-laid ones

"I'm so glad you've finally let me help plan your wedding!" Mother gushed.

"Well, I got the point you wanted to be involved after you asked me for the eighth time at dinner the other night."

"Yes, family dinner. I'm so glad we've been able to start that up again since you gave up volunteering at that shelter."

Her dislike of the soup kitchen was clear from the shape of her mouth.

"I haven't stopped volunteering, Mum. They just found a few extra people and don't need help on a Thursday anymore."

"Well, you'll need to stop going on Wednesdays for a while, too. Then we can have a regular night for planning."

I groaned inwardly. Honestly, the woman could be such hard work.

"Surely we can manage without that?"

"But Wednesday is the only night I am free, what with bridge and your father's card night...."

"Can't you skip cards for a few weeks? Wednesday is the only night I have other plans."

"Lucy," Mother put on her plummiest tone, "Why should I have to make sacrifices in my life for *your* wedding?"

Because this is all your idea and I don't want to do it your way?

"What I do at the soup kitchen is important, Mum. They need people to help feed the homeless..."

"Well, they should round up all the homeless in town and put them in a shelter, use their pensions to—"

"Stop right there. We are not having this conversation again. I will talk to Vanessa and try to get the next *three* Wednesdays free. Other than that, I can't promise anything."

She sniffed and nodded.

"That will do to start with. Now, let's start with some lists..."

I vagued out as she started listing: venue, flowers, bridesmaids, dresses, menus, undergarments. Ew, I was not letting Mother choose my undergarments.

"So, the wedding will be on Valentine's Day," Mum said.

I tuned back in for that.

"Wait, what?" I asked.

"Manners, Lucy. I said Valentine's Day. Next year. Won't it be so lovely, a Valentine's Day wedding?"

"I don't know, isn't it a bit...Hallmark?"

You know, stereotypical and lame.

"Oh no! You know I so desperately wanted a Valentine's Day wedding myself, but well, you know."

I did know. It was quite the scandal. Mother and Father had gotten married in quite a hurry. In December. I was born the following May. If they'd waited for a Valentine's Day wedding, the reason for the rush would have been clear for all to see.

Once again, I felt guilty about my almost-illegitimate status, like it was my fault for daring to be conceived from their pre-marital sex.

"I'm sorry, Mum. Maybe I can talk to Joe about it. We hadn't really talked about a date yet. We're too excited about the engagement for now."

"Yes, the engagement. I'm glad you mentioned it. I've put an announcement in this weekend's newspaper, and there is a high tea at the Country Club for you Saturday next."

"You organised a high tea?"

"Of course, dear, that's the best way to celebrate an engagement. I've arranged for a wishing well, too. That way, you don't have to bother about a registry."

"Mum, I don't even know if Joe will be free that day."

I pulled up my calendar so I could check my own availability.

"But darling, I went to all this effort for you. It was the only time they could fit you in for another four weeks. I had to ask the caterer to fit in an extra event that day."

"Mum, you didn't even check the date with me first! I could have had something on. How am I going to arrange for my friends to be able to get there at such short notice?"

"Never mind that. The Country Club is arranging it all. And we're putting it on as an engagement present to you. You won't say no, will you?"

I sighed. "I'll check with Joe."

"Are you sure you don't mind?" I asked Joe again.

"Of course, I don't mind." He said. "If it means that more people know you are taken, I am perfectly happy."

His smile was radiant as he looped his arm around my waist.

"But you'll have to miss your training session."

"It's only an online training course. They'll run it again next month. I'm sure my boss will understand and re-register me."

"Thank you."

I kissed him gently on the lips.

"You're the best," I said. "Now, how do you feel about a Valentine's Day wedding?"

I pulled my neck down into my shoulders and pulled away from him.

"That's fine with me too." He said.

"Really? Because I think it's a bit stereotypical and naff, but my Mum thinks that it would be really romantic and lovely, and Valentine's Day will fall on a Sunday next year. Most weddings are held on a Saturday so that you don't have to worry about keeping people up all night, but I'm sure people will be able to arrange a day off for Monday if they have enough warning."

"It's absolutely fine if it's what you want."

I chewed on my bottom lip. Was it what I wanted? The main point was that I wanted to marry Joe. It didn't matter whether I was marrying him in a mud pit or on a mountain top, as long as we were married. But it would make Mum happy if we were married on Valentine's Day.

I loved my mum, even if she drove me crazy sometimes. It was a small thing I could do that might make up for all the sacrifices she had made for me.

"Yes, let's see if we can make Valentine's Day work."

February 14, 10:00 a.m.
Tipsy bridesmaids

The doorbell rang right on time.

The hairdresser and make-up artist had arrived. They had exactly forty minutes to get my hair done, and make-up on before the photographer arrived to take the first photos. Of course, the first ones would mostly be set photos, my dress on the mannequin I had bought specifically to keep the dress in shape, then covered with a satin sheet to make sure Joseph didn't see it before I walked down the aisle, my jewellery and my shoes.

The make-up artist set out her brushes while the hairdresser straightened my hair, set it in an elegant bun atop my head and curled the strands she had left free.

My bridesmaids stood in the kitchen talking quietly while I was being styled. I felt a little left out. It seemed like they had more going on together these days than they had with me, and I was the one who had brought them together. I called them over to join me.

"What are you guys talking about?" I asked.

"Oh, just these guys we met at the club a couple nights ago—" Kendall started explaining, but Nora elbowed her in the side.

"Nothing important," Nora said.

"Oh, come on, don't keep secrets from me. I'm the bride!" I said.

The four of them exchanged glances.

"Yeah, we know," Perry said.

"Come on then, tell me," I said.

"Well, we went out on Thursday night." Nora took the lead in telling the story. "To that new club, you know, Nightfeeders? We found ourselves a bunch of high rollers, didn't we, girls?"

The others giggled.

"We sure did," Kendall added.

"This bunch of guys—" Nora started but was interrupted when the hairdresser signalled that I should move over to the make-up artist.

I moved over, and Bridget took my place with the hairdresser.

"So, anyway, these guys." Nora resumed her story. "They bought us drinks all night and were super spunks. We all came away with a phone number."

The others giggled in agreement.

"Sounds like it was a fun night. I'm sorry I missed it."

Because I wasn't invited.

Bridget took pity on me.

"Oh, it wasn't all fun. Remember that other guy that was hanging around, Kendall?"

"Oh, yeah, him," Kendall said with a shudder. "What was with him?"

"He was so wasted," Perry said. "He just kept hanging off all the women in the club."

"I had to wipe his drool off my arm at one point. He was gross."

"I'm pretty sure he licked me."

I grimaced. "Gross. Okay, that's enough of that story now."

Bridget put her hand up to her nose and sneezed. For the first time, I noticed the black rings under her eyes. Thankfully, the make-up artist I selected was skilled enough to hide the shadows. Though now that I looked, the others also had marks under their eyes, and Nora's nose was a bit red.

"Well, I hope that gross guy didn't make you sick," I said.

"Ugh, don't worry, he was gross, but I don't think what he had was catching."

"Put it this way, I don't think the redness around his nose was from sneezing," Kendall said.

The other three brayed with laughter.

Where did I find these girls? The thought popped into my head, and I hastily shoved it away.

They were society girls. My mother had hand-picked them to be my bridesmaids. They all brought their own status to the wedding. They were all from rich families, all old money. They had all had a proper debutante ball at the Country Club. They were the *right people* to be my bridesmaids.

It had been the same for Sky Valley's elite for years. I was a bridesmaid for Kendall's older sister 3 years ago. It's how it works in this town. Of the four bridesmaids, only Bridget hadn't been a bridesmaid before. They all knew the drill.

Which is why it really annoyed me when they started joking around while waiting to get their hair and make-up done.

"Ok!" I called over the din. "Can I have a time check, please?"

"Ten fifty free," Perry said, then started giggling at her slur. "Fifty—thirty—thirty! Three."

Bridget, Kendall and Nora also collapsed in giggles.

This was nearly disastrous for Kendall, who bumped the arm of the hairdresser, resulting in the poor woman jerking away so she didn't burn Kendall's face with the curling iron. That really wouldn't have been good for Kendall. The make-up artist was already going to have a hard job ahead of her. My brother doesn't call her 'Ken doll' for nothing. Kendall has strong features.

"Okay, let's take a break from the bubbles!" I said, glaring at Nora.

Everyone knew it was the role of the maid of honour to keep everyone else sober.

"Yes, Ma'am," Nora said.

She reached for Perry's glass and whisked it away to the kitchen.

"But we've only had one bottle!" Kendall objected. "Before Sharon Gisberg's wedding, three of us polished off four bottles of Dom Perignon."

"And we all know how Sharon Gisberg's marriage went," I said.

"That was hardly the fault of the bridesmaids!" Nora objected.

Bridget sprayed the crumbs of a tuna vol-au-vent across the room as she started laughing. "Well, it was the fault of the bridesmaid she found him—"

"That's enough!" I said. "Can we just get back on topic here? Me! Today is about me! I don't want any horror stories about marriages that barely lasted through the reception or dirty, sleazy guys in clubs."

The four of them clucked and came in to enclose me in a group hug.

"Of course! We're sorry," Nora cooed.

"You look absolutely perfect, even in a bath robe," Kendall added.

"When you walk down the aisle, Joe will have to pinch himself to make sure he isn't dreaming. Once you've got that dress on—"

"You'll be in the wet dreams of some of the teenage boys for a few weeks," Kendall said.

Nora cuffed the back of her scalp.

"Jusht. Booiful." Perry managed.

"Somebody sober her up," I said.

I moved away from my chaos of bridesmaids.

March 11, last year
Choices of Churches

"Are you all ready for the engagement party this weekend?" Mum asked.

It was the first of three Wednesdays I had organised to be free from the soup kitchen to plan the wedding, and I'd just sat down at Mum's dining table.

It was starting already.

"I need to be ready? What do I need to do?" I asked, a hint of panic entering my voice.

"No, dear. You don't need to *do* anything. I was asking if you have your outfit ready. Do you know how you will wear your hair?" Mum said.

"Oh! Now I get you." I said. "I think I'll wear the dress I wore to cousin Melinda's wedding last year. The navy blue with the lace sleeves, remember?"

"Oh yes, that was lovely. You will have your hair up this time, won't you? I do think an updo is much nicer than the wild curls."

The "wild curls" had been perfectly formed ringlets that took my hairdresser over an hour to set, but sure, call them wild curls.

"Yes, I can probably manage something like that," I said.

"Very good. Now let's start with some ideas for the ceremony venue." She said.

I took a deep breath and braced myself.

"Yes, we were talking about that the other day. Do you know the Pioneer's reserve? There's a waterfall and lovely gardens. It would be so beautiful down there. Leila suggested it the other day."

I smiled, thinking of all the beautiful, simple plans we'd

discussed with Leila and Nate.

"Nate said he would register as a celebrant for us."

Mother's wine glass paused in mid-air. From the look on her face, you'd have thought I'd suggested burying Grandma in her daggiest nightie. She deliberately lowered the wine glass and placed it gently on the table.

"Lucy. What foolish ideas has that friend of yours put into your head? Marriages happen in *churches*. The members of our family have been married in churches for centuries, and you, my dear, will not break that tradition."

"But Mum, we don't even go to church," I said. "I think the last time I went was Easter...when I was twelve. Isn't it a bit hypocritical to go to church and make vows in front of God when you don't go any other day of the year?"

This time she picked her wine glass up and had a hearty swig.

"You were baptised and confirmed as a member of the church, and you will be married in a church. I didn't want to bring this into play, but traditionally, the bride's parents will cover the cost of the wedding, so I'd like to have a say in how it is run."

My brain exploded, reformed and exploded again.

"That's very kind of you. But we both work and are paid quite well for our efforts. We can afford to pay for our own wedding. It might not be as big and fancy as you expect, but we can manage well enough."

"Nonsense. You don't want a wedding based on eBay finds and reject shop bonbonniere. You want class. I take it you aren't planning to divorce Joe and get married again, so make it a great one. One that you will be able to remember for your whole life. That will be worth telling your grandchildren about."

"Does anyone plan to divorce someone before they are even married?" I asked stupidly.

"Lucy, be serious."

I closed my eyes and took a deep breath.

"Alright, what suggestions do you have? I will talk to Joe

about it. The decisions should be made by both of us. It is his wedding too."

She sniffed. "Well, if you must. But it seems to me that the men don't usually give a fig about their weddings and are perfectly happy for all the decisions to be made for them."

"That might be the case, but I want to check with Joe." I tried to be firm with her. "What are the suggestions?"

"Do you remember the church where Aunt Erin was married? I think you were about six at the time."

"Oh, yes, I was the flower girl. That was a lovely church. The stained-glass windows were spectacular."

"Yes, that one. I've contacted the priest there already. They generally only have a morning service there on a Sunday, so I've had him pencil you in for the afternoon..."

"Whoa, hang on. I just said I would need to check with Joe."

"Yes, but I contacted the priest three days ago. You have to get onto these things quickly, Lucy. It isn't like those American romance novels you read. It takes more than a month to put a wedding together, and venues book out over a year in advance.

"St Columba's was the fourth church I called for you, and the first one that had any availability."

Four churches. She had called four churches without even asking if I was interested in any of them. Lord save me.

I blew a breath out of my mouth and fluffed up the wayward bits of hair around my face.

"Okay. Have you organised a tour of the church?"

She nodded.

"Yes, I will go out and take a look tomorrow. They have a service at 11 a.m. on Thursday, I won't go to the service, but the minister agreed to show me around afterwards."

"Mum! I can't go to that. I'll be at work. I could possibly work it out with a bit of notice, but tomorrow?"

My heart thundered in my ears, and my cheeks burned from my temper kept barely in check.

38

"Don't worry about it at all. I'll make sure it's all sorted. Consider it my gift to you. Organising all the big things, so you just have to worry about choosing your dress and getting there on time."

I could see that the argument for control of my wedding was not going to be won in one night. Or on my own.

I closed my eyes, took a deep breath, tamped down my irritation and agreed to let her look at the church.

"Lei-laaaa," I mock-wailed down the phone line. I was flopped face down on my bed, still in my work clothes, shoes kicked off at the door of my two-bedroom unit. "What am I going to do?"

"Lucy, honey, I've just gotten home from the shelter, and we got slammed. I do not have the brain power to tease out the problem. Start at the beginning and give it to me straight."

I heard the clack of glass hitting a table, followed by the squeak her favourite armchair made when she flopped down in it.

"My mother is taking over my wedding."

"O-kay. Give me more."

"She called four churches, four! She's visiting one tomorrow, and she's chosen the date and told me that all I will have to choose myself is my gown. She's going to do everything!"

The wail in my voice was real now, and it had steadily risen in pitch. I rolled with the squeal and screamed into my pillow.

"I thought you didn't want to get married in a church."

Leila completely ignored my histrionics.

"I didn't, I don't, but it's a family tradition. She won't let me get married in a garden."

"Lucy, honey, you're an adult. You can do what you want."

"I know." I wailed. "But she said she's paying, and the planning will be our wedding gift, and it would be good to

39

just have it all done, but it would also be good to be able to have a say in it."

"I know," she said. "Why don't you convince her to hire a wedding planner to work with? Won't she have to work around all her social engagements anyway?"

I thought about it for a moment. "That's true, you're right, that could work."

"I do have good ideas from time to time."

I laughed.

"Now, did you also say something about a date?" Leila asked with interest.

"Oh, did I not tell you last week? I must have tried to block it from my mind. Valentine's Day. Next year."

She squealed. "That's adorable! A Valentine's wedding."

"You reckon?" I asked.

"Of course!" She said.

A weight lifted from my chest. She certainly would know.

"That is such a short time to plan a wedding, though. Dresses can take ages to arrive, and then there's the engagement party..."

"Oh, don't worry, Mum has that sorted too." My gut clenched up.

"What?"

"There will be a high tea at the Country Club to celebrate our engagement next Saturday. Mum organised it without even checking whether we were available. Or anyone else. Apparently, the Country Club are organising the invitations too. You have to come! Please tell me you can come?"

"Next Saturday, hang on."

I heard the couch springs release her weight, followed by paper flipping, and I imagined her flipping through her ever-present diary.

"Yep, what time?"

"I don't even know! High tea is usually around three, right?"

"I cannot say I have been to enough high teas to know what time they are usually held."

She gave a huge yawn.

"Oh, Leila, I'm sorry, it's after ten. You must have been run off your feet without me tonight, and now I'm keeping you up. Let's catch up in the next few days."

"Tomorrow night?" She asked.

I groaned. "I can't, family dinner."

"You had to go there tonight, and you still have to have family dinner tomorrow? That sucks."

"I know. What's worse is that my brother has managed to arrange a uni lecture on Thursdays, so he's gotten out of it for the next six months. She is totally inflexible and won't change so that he can make it, though, will she? No. I just have to come alone, and she's all gushy about how he will be an engineer in two more semesters, and he doesn't get any shade about it. Yet Joe and I hear every week about how she so graciously let me skip that one time when we first met. It's like she thinks it was only at her mercy that we got the opportunity to get together."

I was panting by the time I finished my spiel.

"Girl, you need to let some of that go." Leila yawned again. "Friday then?"

"Yes, Friday, five-thirty. Margaritas?"

"Heck, yes. Good night. Love you."

"Love you, too."

I disconnected the call and sighed. Leila was a legend.

I was so lucky to have her in my life.

February 14, 11:31 a.m.
Herding drunken cats

"Will you just get in the damn car?" I cried.

We should have left the house at 11:30 exactly. All the 'before' photos had been taken, my parents had been and gone for the daughter photos, the obligatory photos of the garter going on and the maid of honour lacing me into the damn dress were done, we were due for glamour shots in the church gardens in half an hour, and we still needed to stop and pick up our lunch.

The photographer had already zipped off to take photos of Joseph and his groomsmen. We needed to leave.

Nora and Kendall were chaperoning a barely upright Perry out of the front door, and Bridget was stumbling along herself.

"What the hell is wrong with you three? I'd ask if someone rufie'd the Champagne, but I drank from the same bottle. Have you deliberately taken something?"

"Not since Tuesday!" Nora giggled.

As Bridget stepped past me, I noticed a thin sheen of perspiration on her forehead.

Somehow, they all looked slightly dishevelled, despite the hours put into their appearances.

"Sweet baby cheeses," I muttered, watching Kendall manhandling Perry into the limousine.

"Hey, Miss Sandy," my elderly neighbour called out.

Sandy had died almost 6 years earlier, but Mr Kroger was blind as a bat and half senile. It didn't matter how many times I told him my name; he never remembered.

"Have you seen the news this morning?"

"No, Mr Kroger, I've been a bit busy. I'm actually just getting ready to go out. I'll have to chat to you later."

"Oh, but Miss Sandy. It's terrible news. Lots of people are getting sick, they say." His blind eyes scoured a spot over my left shoulder as he spoke. "Really bad, they say. People are dead but still walking around the place."

I rolled my eyes. "Really, Mr Kroger? That's really interesting." He'd probably gotten the channels mixed up and had listened to the start of a horror movie instead of the morning news. "I have to go now, but you keep watching and see how that pans out."

Mad old guy.

"Yeah, yeah, I'll do that," he said. "You be careful now, Miss Sandy."

When I turned back, I was relieved to find all of the bridesmaids finally contained in the limousine. I collected my skirts and piled myself and them into the car.

We finally left home, 10 minutes behind schedule.

March 12, last year
A-3

"I can't believe you are willing to put up with all of that for the rest of your life. Are you sure?" I asked Joe.

I held my hands up to my face before turning to him. I opened a little gap in my fingers to peek at his face.

Joe changed gears, and lanes, before answering me.

"Thankfully, Luce, I'm marrying you, not your mother. I will not have to live with her.

"I can only imagine what your teenage years were like."

"I try to forget them. You are so good to me."

He took his hand off the gearstick and grabbed mine from where I had dropped it onto my lap.

"I can't wait until we're going home to *our* place after family dinner."

"Well, it looks like it will only be eleven months away."

"Excellent. Where shall we live, your place or mine?" He asked.

"Hmm, what about *our* place," I said.

He cocked his head at me as he turned a corner.

"Well, I've got some savings, and you're in finance, so I bet you've got some too. We could buy a place and then move into it together. And then furnish it using the funds from the engagement wishing well Mum has organised."

I went from being excited about the house to bummed about the wishing well. I hated the idea of asking people for money. It seemed so common to me, yet the people in Mum and Dad's upper echelons of society thought it was just fine.

"Well, I'm sure that will be lovely. Maybe we can use it for a nice piece of art and share a picture of it as a thank you to the people who contributed."

As always, he raised my spirits.

"That is a great idea."

"So was the one about the house.

"What should we get? A bigger unit, a house, an apartment?"

"An apartment?" I laughed. "There is only one residential building in this town that you could consider to be an apartment block, and it's the residential care village. I don't think marriage will put us straight into that category."

He laughed back. "That wasn't really an answer."

"A house. With a yard for veggies and chickens and a cat and a dog and an axolotl."

"An axolotl? Shall we put a couple of zebra fish in a tank, too, so we can say we have pets from A-Z?"

I laughed and punched him gently on the shoulder.

The car squeaked as he wrenched the handbrake on.

"Well, for tonight, my lady, let us stay at *yours*, and we can get to researching about *ours*."

March 21, last year
Guests who weren't invited

"And how are you, Leila? Marriage seems to be agreeing with you. You are positively glowing!" Mum said.

"Oh, thank you. Yes, Nate and I are quite happy and settling into our house." Leila said.

"How long has it been?" Mum asked before popping a canape in her mouth.

"Four months now." Leila smiled.

"Oh, so it could well be a *different* sort of glow I see on your cheeks? The expectant one?" Mum asked.

My cheeks flushed in embarrassment. "Mum! You can't ask someone that."

Leila laughed it off, but the laughter felt brittle.

"No, we aren't expecting yet, but we are considering adding to our family in the next year or so."

Her smile grew bright as I passed her one of the glasses of sparkling wine I'd nabbed from one of the circulating waiters.

I gulped half of mine. I hadn't thought the social awkwardness could get worse after the situation at the door earlier.

Leila and Nate had arrived just after 3:00 p.m. and been asked for their invitation at the door to the function room. It had taken several minutes for me to hear the hubbub. Leila asked the doorman to find me for my approval to enter. He insisted that he could only allow her entrance with my mother's approval. Mother was still upstairs preparing to make a grand entrance once she was sure ninety per cent of the guests had arrived.

Finally, Leila got my attention, and I had to explain to the door man that she was my personal guest and that her invitation must have been lost in the mail.

"How did she know about the party then?" The doorman

asked.

"I told her about it," I said. "I called her on the telephone and gave her the details. Just let them in."

"Very well."

He stepped aside to allow them to enter and asked the next waiting couple for their invitation.

A crowd had gathered in the corridor behind Leila and Nate, and I hurried them away from the doorway, so they didn't become victim to the hot stares of rich impatience.

"I'm so sorry," I said to Leila. "You really didn't receive an invitation?"

She smiled a little sadly. "Nope."

I growled, "I should have known better than to leave it to Mother."

"You'd best be sure she gives you the list of wedding guests before those invitations go out."

I groaned and held my hand against my stomach. It had lurched against my tight, lace bodice.

"You know, I did end up getting a licence to officiate weddings. We could all go out to the garden now and get the whole thing over with." Nate said.

"Where's Joe?" I said before thinking. "No, I can't do that. She's so excited about planning the wedding."

I thought a moment longer.

"You know, if I got pregnant...she'd be inclined to bring the wedding forward. It would shorten the whole period of trauma for us all."

Leila didn't laugh.

"Don't even joke about that. You know, I do keep telling you, you can do whatever you want. You are an adult."

"I know, but it's just hard to disappoint her."

She smiled, but Mother drew our attention by making her expected grand entrance before we could continue the conversation.

She smiled and gushed at people as she moved past the waiting crowd and into the room.

She had zeroed in on us and moved straight to the

conversation of additional embarrassment.

"So, Mum..." I racked my brain for a conversation point that would break the awkward pause. "How about you talk us through your tour of the church the other day?"

Her smile broadened, and she collected a glass of sparkling wine for herself. I checked the level of my and Leila's glasses, probably enough to keep us going for a few more minutes.

"Well! St Columba's is just lovely. So quaint. There are a few areas that have fallen into disrepair. I've arranged for your father to make a sizable donation."

"Oh, Mum! I'm so sorry you've had to do that. Was it really that bad? We could have found somewhere else to hold the ceremony."

"Oh, nonsense," she said. "I'm sure it was the only church that was free that day."

I exchanged a quick glance with Leila. "But we don't have to get married on the fourteenth of February. We can pick a different day."

"No, no, no. Valentine's Day will be so lovely, and I just want you to have a wedding day worth telling your grandchildren about."

She smiled at me. I tried not to groan.

Leila, bless her, interrupted the moment.

"Oh, Dorothea, I think I see your husband waving."

She pointed across the room to where Dad was gesticulating wildly.

Mum huffed out a breath.

"Oh, I have told him so many times that is not a polite way to get someone's attention. Do excuse me, dears."

She squeezed Leila's arm as she smiled and disappeared, leaving a wake of rose and geranium perfume in her path.

"Oh my goodness, I'm so sorry," I said to Leila and Nate. "I can't believe she said that to you. Asking someone when they will have kids is so not polite."

Leila tried to laugh it off, but there was a tightness around the corners of her eyes that told me I wasn't getting the full story.

I decided to let it slide. This was not the place to have a conversation about fertility. Not that I cared about turning the focus away from me at my engagement party, it was just that there were so many people at the party I would not be comfortable having around for such a conversation.

For example, cousin Kendall.

The lanky, long-faced blonde tottered towards us and squealed.

"Lucy! I'm so excited that you're getting married!" She dragged out the last word to 'Marrr-eeeeeed'.

I pasted fake excitement on my face to match her own. "Me too!"

"And that man you chose, what a spunk."

She licked her finger and wiped it in the air to mime a sizzle.

"Well." Joe's voice came from behind me. "I happen to think I'm getting a pretty good deal myself."

I felt his breath on my neck as he rested his chin on my shoulder and snaked a hand around my waist. I turned my face towards him to place a kiss neatly on his lips with a noisy smacking.

"Where have you been? I lost you when Leila and Nate got here."

"I was waylaid by your brother. He wanted to talk to me about a video game tournament he is setting up with a couple of mates."

Kendall sniggered. "Oh, is Lyon still doing that? Little video game nights with his mates?"

"Yeah, he is, actually. He has even managed to get into a few paid tournaments now."

Kendall looked as if her long face had been slapped full length with a fish.

Only when I turned my head to see if my friend saw her comical face too did I realise that Leila and Nate had slipped away. I decided to let them be and find them again later.

I completed my third searching lap of the room an hour later. Once again, my search was fruitless. Leila and Nate, it seemed, had left the party.

I found myself wishing for a moment that we had left with them. I spent another moment wishing we had let Nate marry Joe and me in the garden so we could have the whole thing over with. The next moment, I was in Joe's arms, there was a wine glass in my hands, and I decided life was too short to worry.

February 14, 11:42 a.m.
Bridesmaid betrayal

"Bridget? Are you okay to go in and get the lunch?"

Bridget blinked at me owlishly. I was pretty certain she was not usually a morning drinker.

"Huh? Yeah, of course."

The limousine double parked in the street outside the supermarket, and my youngest bridesmaid climbed out, stumbling only slightly.

As the door thumped shut, the driver pulled away to drive around the block as we'd arranged. One lap around the block should take a little less than 5 minutes and be more than enough time for Bridget to collect the platters of sandwiches from the deli section at the back of the supermarket and meet us back on the street.

I had initially planned for someone to come out with them, but they hadn't returned my calls to confirm that morning, so I'd changed my plans on the fly. I hoped desperately that there wouldn't be any sudden pasta sauce jar disasters for Bridget to be caught in on her way through the store.

A deep, guttural groan echoed down the length of the limo.

Nora and Kendall had been sitting with Perry propped up between them, but Perry appeared to have doubled over, and the groan turned into retching.

"Perry?" Kendall asked, "are you okay?"

"Ughnnnhhhnnngggg."

I was unable to decipher any clear syllables from the groan. I looked at each of the three members of the bridal party still sharing the limo with me. Kendall's eyes were glassy, and tendrils of hair were stuck to her temples with perspiration. Perry was still folded over. Nora didn't look much better than Perry, her arm was clutched across her abdomen, and her face showed an expression of pain.

I pulled the skirt and train of my *very* expensive bridal gown close to my ankles and well away from the potential splashback of any bridesmaid oral expulsions.

I was not walking down the aisle with bodily fluids adorning my gown.

The fear for my dress took a backseat to the fear for my bridesmaid as Perry grunt-groaned again. She tensed, her upper body flipping upright and her legs straightening. It was a weird distortion of the plank pose, with her body braced by her head against the back of the seat and her heels against the floor of the vehicle.

"Guys? Is Perry...okay?"

I expected a swift response from Kendall, who was a nurse, but she seemed completely oblivious to our friend's pain. Instead, Kendall's limbs were thrashing about, her hands hitting the windows with painful-sounding thuds.

"Nora?"

All the while, the driver seemed oblivious to his passengers' plight and continued down the block.

The privacy shield was up, and goodness knows what he had heard from his back seat in the past. This could be a standard pre-wedding outing for him, for all I knew.

A grunt and splash punctuated the emptying of Nora's stomach, thankfully well away from the hem of my dress.

Perry's body relaxed, and she slumped against the seat, her head lolling against Nora's shoulder. A small trickle of blood seeped from the corner of her mouth and onto Nora. I watched in horror as it moved down Nora's décolletage and seeped into the neckline of her dress.

"Perry, are you okay?"

Perry's head swung up at the sound of my voice. Her eyes were unfocussed, and the bright red of her blood clashed with her coral lipstick.

She looked pale beneath her foundation, the splashes of

blush seemed too bright, and her mascara had run. Her eyeliner had also smeared, leaving broad smudges where before there had been fine lines.

"Kendall?" My voice wavered, and I resented the fear I heard, so I turned from questioning to demanding. "Kendall? If this is some kind of prank, I am so not impressed. I bet Bridget will be upset that she is missing out on the fun. Did one of you hide a camera so you could take photos of me while you pulled this stunt?"

Kendall let out a squeak that could have concealed laughter.

I shook my head and grimaced. "You had so better have someone organised to meet us to fix up your make-up before the next round of photos."

I crossed my arms over my chest and tried not to wrinkle my brow.

"You'd better have a plan to get that 'blood' out of Nora's dress too."

I was so furious that I couldn't look at them anymore.

I knew that Kendall was one for pranks, and I suspected I had been getting on their nerves a little in the last few months, but a prank like this on someone's wedding day was just plain cruel.

I turned back to them as the limo pulled back around onto the street with the supermarket.

"And I hope...."

My hopes for no similar pranks to be played on my husband-to-be died on my lips as my gaze fell back on my bridesmaids.

None of them were showing the chagrin I would have expected from people caught out in their prank. None of them were even cracking a smile or appeared to be laughing at their little joke.

On closer observation, none of them even appeared to be breathing.

March 22, last year
Fertile grounds?

"I still can't believe you just left the party." I said to Leila, "I'm kind of bummed that I couldn't do the same myself."

Leila sank back into her armchair—the springs creaked as she relaxed—and cradled her glass of white wine.

"I'm sorry," she said, "It was just too much. First the joke about the pregnancy and then your mother...I'm just a bit hormonal, I guess."

"Don't apologise, it's fine. I'm sure you saw an opportunity and just had to take it."

"It was literally a break in the crowd leading straight to the door." She laughed a little. "I'm so embarrassed, though. It's so not like me to run like that. It must be part of coming off the pill."

I sipped my wine and studied her face. She looked tired.

"How long ago did you stop taking it?" I asked.

"About two months." She squinted her left eye in thought. "I've had one period since then, and it was epic, but before I got it, oh my gosh, I was such a crazy, cranky cow."

We laughed.

"How long do they say it usually takes to get pregnant?"

"It can happen straight away, apparently, but not for us. They say not to worry until you've been trying for at least six months without luck, and let me tell you, we are trying very hard."

I crunched my eyebrows together.

"Too much information!" I half-sang.

She laughed.

The boys chose that moment to walk into the room, Nate

holding a large wooden chopping board with dips, cabana, cheese and crackers.

"Mmm mmm, that looks good," Leila said. "Oh, and the food looks tasty too."

We all laughed at that.

I filed away the information about pregnancy for future reference, and we began our board game night in happy companionship.

February 14, 11:50 a.m.
Driver

"Kendall? Nora? Perry?"

Their bodies were still slumped against the limo seat, their limbs tangled together.

I had never seen a dead body before. I had no idea what to do. Seconds that felt like decades ticked by. Shops rolled past the windows as we moved, shaded out by the heavy tinting and looking as surreal as the women's bodies in front of me.

A foul smell emanated from them, and the shock to my nose pulled me out of my stupor.

Holy beans, I bet this has never happened to anyone on their wedding day. Three dead bridesmaids. Three dead bridesmaids!

"I need to call an ambulance or the police or something." I knew my babbling was falling on deaf ears, but I needed to fill the silence with some noise.

I quietly cursed myself for not wanting any music playing in the car on the way to the ceremony. A little quiet jazz right now would really settle my mind.

"Phone. A phone. I need a phone."

I closed my eyes so I could think without looking at the horror in front of me. My small clutch was in the boot of the limo, sitting next to the box holding our bouquets. My phone was nestled neatly in the clutch, on silent so it wouldn't disturb my big day.

I knew Kendall had stuffed her phone in her bra before leaving. I opened my eyes and studied her bust line. The phone had moved as she'd been thrashing, and I could see the top quarter of it poking out of her dress, but wild horses wouldn't get me pulling that out.

The privacy screen in the limo was still up, but there was a phone for me to call the driver.

I picked it up and hoped it would connect straight through. It did.

"Yes, ladies, how can I help you?"

"It's just the one lady, actually," my voice quavered. "Lucy. Umm, my bridesmaids, those who are still here anyway, well, it looks like they aren't here anymore."

"Huh?" The driver asked.

"I think they're dead!" Despite my efforts to stay calm, I shrieked.

"Who's dead?"

"Kendall, Perry and Nora. They had a weird seizure thing, and now they're not moving. I don't think they're breathing."

I lurched forward in my seat as the driver slammed on the brakes.

The bodies of my bridesmaids moved with the abrupt stop too, but the continued rustling of chiffon made me look towards the front of the vehicle.

I thought the bodies were settling, but I saw the distinct movement of the bodies I had formerly declared dead.

"Oh, thank goodness, Kendall is moving, maybe they're okay after all, but they don't look well. I think we'll need an ambulance."

My brain zoomed ahead to the next stop along the way. I wasn't going to be able to take the limo any further, and I wouldn't need one anyway: Kendall, Perry and Nora weren't going to be part of the wedding day from here. They'd probably given themselves alcohol poisoning with the Champagne breakfast. I knew I'd seen Perry's hip flask out, and goodness only knew what she'd had in it.

I was suddenly angry at them. They knew how important my wedding day was. I'd been focused on nothing but making sure the day was absolutely perfect for the last 8 months. How dare they stuff it up like this!

Perry lurched upward, throwing Nora and Kendall's

limp bodies off her shoulders to slump down on the seat behind her. An eerie groan came from Nora after her face hit the seat.

The privacy screen behind their seat started to roll down with a quiet whirr, and the driver's hat and eyes appeared slowly.

"What do you mean? First, they're dead, and now they're not?" He asked before the window had revealed his entire face.

Perry's head turned at the sound, tilting sideways to look at the driver.

"Yeezus! What happened to her?" He bounced back away from the bridesmaid.

"I don't know, bad moonshine, I suspect," I said.

"I have never seen moonshine do that to a person. Did you see her eyes?"

"No?"

A beeping car horn from behind the limo started a chorus and drew us back to the relevant details.

"Right, I can't keep the car here, and that one definitely needs an ambulance." He turned his attention back to the road. "There's a place up there I can park."

He put the car back in drive, and the car rolled forward. The chorus of horns eased as we started to move.

Kendall's arm started to twitch, and she made a grumbling, gurgling sound as she struggled to bring herself upright.

A small voice told me I should help them, but a louder one told me they'd brought it on themselves, and I shouldn't risk my appearance.

The limo moved slowly towards a bus stop and pulled in. I heard the clicking of indicators. The driver had probably put the hazard lights on.

"Okay, have you called an ambulance?" the driver asked.

"How would I have called an ambulance? I don't have a phone on me. Do you think this dress has a hidden phone pocket underneath the beading?"

"Okay, okay, I'll call then." He turned back to the front of the vehicle and fished his phone from somewhere.

Perry was still watching him, her head cocked on an angle that looked uncomfortable.

"Perry, how are you feeling?" I asked, leaning forward. "What was in your hip flask?"

Her head turned to me, but her neck remained at a crooked angle. Her eyes appeared slowly, but I could see they were bloodshot even from a few metres away. When both eyes came into view, I realised they weren't bloodshot; the whites of her eyes were completely red. They had sunken back slightly into her skull, and her irises roamed, unfixed, independent of each other.

"Perry?"

Kendall levered herself upright in jerky movements by lurching up a little and wedging her body between the seat and Perry's back. I wondered if she somehow injured her arms as they dangled limply beside her body.

Nora stayed prone.

"I need an ambulance, or maybe two. How many sick have you got back there?" The driver asked.

"Three," I said.

"I've got three unconscious women in the back of my limo. I don't know what happened. The bride just told me they'd passed out. Yes, I said the bride, you know, the one in the big white dress at the wedding?"

I ignored the last bit. "It looked like they had seizures, one of them vomited."

"Seizures and vomiting, apparently. Here, I'll patch you through the car stereo, then the bride can talk to you directly."

He tapped on his phone screen and told me to pick up the phone handset and press 4 to put the call on speaker.

"Hello? Are you the bride?" The voice of the emergency dispatcher was calm and soothing.

"Yes, yes. Lucy, my name is Lucy."

"Okay, Lucy. Can you tell me who is sick and what

happened?"

I explained the last few minutes of horror to the woman.

"Alright, and how do they seem now? Can you check someone's pulse for me?"

"No, I can't get any closer to them. There's a mess."

"A mess? You can't get through a mess?"

Righteous indignation straightened my spine.

"Lady, are you married? Did you wear jeans and sneakers on your wedding day? I'm in a six-thousand-dollar designer bridal gown and seventeen hundred-dollar Louboutin shoes. I am not risking getting vomit on them."

"I'll do it."

The limo driver volunteered with a definite ring of reluctance in his voice.

He shifted from the driver's seat, and I saw him move in front of the car in the snatches of the windscreen that were visible between the other women. The passenger door beside Nora opened but halted when the driver felt the woman's weight fall against it.

He reached an arm through the gap in the door and pressed against her shoulder, pushing her limp body back into the limo so he could open the door fully.

"Ma'am, are you still there?" The emergency operator asked.

I'd forgotten that she was still connected.

"Yes! Yes, we're here. The driver is just with the others now."

He stood outside the limo with his arm outstretched, keeping his body far away from Nora's while he pressed the index finger of his right hand against her neck.

"I can't feel anything. Where are you supposed to touch anyway?"

"I don't think you'll feel anything with her head slumped like that. Lift it up," I said.

The dispatcher spoke up. "Place your first two fingers against the person's throat, just to the side of her windpipe. If the neck is flexed, it may be difficult to feel a pulse. Try

60

flexing the head back against the seat and then try."

I could sense the tension rolling off the man as he reached into the limo and flexed Nora's head back with both hands.

"I'm not feeling anything," he said, poking his fingers against her throat.

"You're moving your hand too fast. You need to hold your fingers still for a few seconds. How are you going to feel anything if you keep moving them?"

He turned his head and glared at me.

"Or she could have a weak pulse that he can't detect." The calm voice came through the car speakers. "Can you check the next lady?"

He placed a foot inside the limo and reached out to Kendall. Repeating the attempt to find a pulse, he touched her neck, pausing this time before moving his fingers to check another location on her throat.

"I can't find a pulse on this one either," he said, "but her fingers are twitching, and she turned her head to look at me before."

"Okay, I'll make a note of that. Can you give me her name?"

I obliged.

"And you said there was a third lady as well. How is she doing?"

Perry was on the seat, her head moving from side to side, groaning quietly.

"She's alive," I said.

"Sir, are you near enough to her to try for a pulse?"

"I don't think I need to—she's moving."

"Okay, what else can you tell me about their condition?"

"Kendall's eyes are bloodshot. Like, completely bloodshot, no white there at all. And she doesn't seem to be able to focus."

"Okay, and is that all of them or just Kendall?"

"I don't know," I said.

"Sir, is there any chance you can check?"

His shoulders squeezed up and then dropped with his sharp intake of breath.

"Okay."

A commotion came from outside the limo.

A voice called. "Whoa, get a look at this. These bridesmaids are wrecked already!"

The limo driver shooed them away and shut the door to give my irresponsible, unconscious bridesmaids some privacy.

He checked Nora's eyes while he was hovering over her. "This one has bloodshot eyes too, but not as bad."

He moved over to Perry in a half shuffle, hunched over now that he was entirely in the vehicle.

He reached his arms towards her face, placing one hand on her forehead and using the other to pry apart her eyelids.

"This one, is it Kerry?"

"Perry."

"Perry. One of her eyes is really red. The other isn't as bad."

I couldn't see all of what happened next, but his body lurched, and he cried out as his body jerked forward over Kendall and Perry. There was a rustling, a wet slurp and a spray of blood across the front of the vehicle.

"What's happening?" The emergency dispatcher didn't sound quite as calm as she had earlier.

I swallowed back the bile that rose in my throat. "It looked like they attacked him."

His body convulsed and slumped down, then flopped back.

My eyes flicked between the gouge of flesh missing from his throat, the blood smeared across Kendall's face, Nora bending forward to reach for the driver's leg, and Perry gnawing on the driver's detached arm.

Yep, that was it. I was out of there.

I unclicked my seatbelt and hurled myself across the seat to the rear door handle. I flung the door open and scrambled, paying no mind to my dress or heels, across the seat and out of the limo of death.

I slammed the door behind me, catching the tail of my cathedral train. I turned my body and heaved to free the train from the door. The sweet sound of tearing satin and tulle heralded my freedom from the terror of my bridesmaids.

I heaved a few deep breaths and realised that the limo's engine was still running.

I had to lock them in!

I hustled around to the front of the limo, ignoring the catcalls of the gathering crowd.

I wrenched open the driver's door and reached in, momentarily forgetting that the privacy screen was down. An arm snaked forward as I grabbed the keys and tried to yank them from the ignition.

They wouldn't come out.

Unthinking, I'd forgotten to turn the engine off.

A head, Perry's, followed the arm through to the front of the vehicle.

"Hello? Is anyone still there?" The dispatcher managed before I twisted the keys out, shutting off the engine and the Bluetooth connection with it.

March 25, last year

Undermining

"Right, now that the engagement party is sorted, we can get onto the bridal party," Mum said.

"Yes, I'll have..."

"Now, I know you'll say you want Leila as your matron of honour."

"Well, yes, she's my closest friend. And Joe will probably want Nate as a groomsman."

Since we couldn't have him marry us as we wanted him to.

I chided myself for being petty.

"Well, that's a lovely plan, but you do have to think about her wanting a family. What if she's pregnant by then? If she gets pregnant in the next couple of months, she could end up being near her due date. You wouldn't want her to go into labour. It would ruin your day!"

I contemplated that for a moment. I couldn't imagine being heavily pregnant, but surely it wouldn't go well with bridesmaid duties.

"That is a good point, but I would still like to have her as my matron of honour. If she gets pregnant, we can work out a plan from there. I'll have a backup, or we'll have both Leila and Nate, and they can both drop out, so the parties will still be even."

I thought the offered solution was sound, but Mum pouted.

"What do you mean, a backup? You can't have a backup bridesmaid. That just isn't polite. It isn't like the murder mystery birthday party you had when you were fourteen. We can't just have a *bridesmaid* reserve list."

"Mum, that's not what I said. I said, let's have them both. *If* she gets pregnant, is close to her due date and doesn't feel up to it, we'll ask both of them if they want to step back from bridal party duties."

"Hrrmph, well. I don't know how you expect me to be able to find a gown for her that will work…"

"I'm sure the people at the bridal shop will be able to help. They've probably had the same problem before. I'll even buy two dresses for her if it makes you happy."

She made a note in the wedding binder she'd compiled, which flashed my memory.

"Did you talk to any of the wedding planners I suggested?" I asked, silently praising Leila-my-saviour.

Mum didn't look up from the binder. "Yes. The first was too inexperienced, and the second had plenty of experience but not in the type of wedding we want to put together. The third was okay but much too expensive."

"Joe and I are happy to pay for the cost of the planner to make things easier for you. You've had to put in so much—"

She held up a hand and looked at me then.

"Nonsense, I will not hear of it. I'm doing this as a labour of love for you. The time is no trouble at all." She smiled. "I just want to make everything as perfect for you as possible and give you a wedding—"

"—worth telling my grandchildren about." I finished. "I know."

I held in a sigh with herculean effort.

"I'm glad you understand." She glanced at the clock. "Heavens, we really haven't got as far along in this planning as I thought we would. It's nearly nine-thirty. I'll have to stop to watch the late news in a moment."

Relief that the ordeal was over flooded through my tight muscles.

"I will need you to come back next Wednesday, though. We still have so much to do." She said.

All of the previously loosened muscles wrenched

themselves tighter than before. I could sense the oncoming tension headache.

"Mum, I can't. I have commitments every Wednesday. Vanessa had to go to a great deal of trouble to cover my last three shifts. It isn't fair to her. And Leila has had to pick up some of the slack too."

"They will be fine without you for another week. Your tablecloths, however, will not pick themselves."

My head spun on that one. "Tablecloths? What on earth are the options for tablecloths that I have to choose from?"

"Well, you'll have to choose whether you want linen or damask. Plain white, textured or a colour.

"Personally, I wouldn't choose a colour. Pure white is the best option for the cleanest-looking tables. There are some lovely prints, though."

I'm doing this to marry Joe. The rest is just details.

"Why don't you email me pictures of the options, and I'll take a look at them with Joe. We can choose together." *And share the pain.* "I do have to head off now, though. It's getting quite late."

"Yes, dear, of course." We both stood and moved to the door. "I'll see you tomorrow night for family dinner, and we can talk more about the bridal party."

"Sure thing, Mum. Good night."

Thank goodness Joe is coming to dinner tomorrow. I could really use the backup.

February 14, 11:55 a.m.
Man-eaters

Although the time in the back of the limousine with my three bridesmaids felt like it had lasted a decade, we'd only driven three-quarters of the way around the block back to the supermarket.

So, I was down two bridesmaids and a maid of honour. That was definitely something *not* to tell my grandchildren.

Wondering what in the name of all that is holy had happened to those three, I tucked the limo keys against the windscreen wiper. My hoop skirt bubbled out behind me, and I thanked my remaining lucky stars that wedding cars were kept clean and there was no dirt to mar my dress.

I walked around the bonnet to find that we had pulled into a bus stop. The indicators were still blinking in unison around the vehicle. The car was definitely a hazard now.

My stomach lurched as my imagination reproduced the image of the three bridesmaids setting on him, and I made sure I didn't look in through the windscreen as I walked around. I didn't need to see that a second time.

The dispatch operator would testify that I wasn't responsible for the injuries to the driver. I couldn't even remember his name. Joe would know. He'd arrange for a bouquet of flowers to be sent to the family after the honeymoon. Not that his fate was our fault.

Sirens echoed down the street, and red and blue lights strobed across the beads of my dress, sending scatterings of light across the ground and limo.

The vehicle stopped in the road next to the front of the limo, and a paramedic approached me.

"You would be Lucy?"

"Yep. Listen, have you got all the details from my call?"

The paramedic cocked her head at me. "Yeah."

"Good. I don't have much more to tell you, and my other bridesmaid is at the supermarket. Let me just grab my clutch, and I'll be off to get her. Can you just grab those keys and click the boot for me?"

The paramedic responded automatically. She picked up the keys and walked the length of the car on the driver's side as I walked down the passenger side.

The boot popped open, and I assessed the contents. I heard the paramedic talking to me but tuned her out as I made plans.

The bouquets, my overnight bag and my clutch, containing my phone, were tucked in neatly. I dug through the blooms to grab my clutch purse, hooked the wrist strap into place, and then pulled out my bouquet. Bridget would need to hold mine during the ceremony, so it wasn't really worth picking up hers.

I spotted the esky, reached in for a chilled bottle of water and took a few big gulps. It settled my nerves and staved off dehydration. I set my shoulders, nodded once and turned to the footpath.

"Wait!" The paramedic raised her voice enough that she caught my attention.

"What's the problem? You can probably figure out that I have somewhere to be, and now I have to work out how to get there."

"Don't you want to stay and find out how your friends are? We can send someone else to find your other bridesmaid and bring her back here."

"They are not my friends. Friends do not get uncontrollably drunk on your wedding day and try to tear your limo driver limb from limb."

The shock sent her face blank.

"Be careful with them. They really are man-eaters."

I turned and clipped down the street towards the supermarket and Bridget.

March 26, last year

Tarragon potatoes

"How are the potatoes, dear?" Mother asked.

"Oh yes, quite lovely, dear," Dad said. "What have you done?"

"I added tarragon," Mother said proudly.

"Is that what's giving them that licorice-y flavour?" Joe asked.

Mother beamed. She loves it when someone can pick the different flavours in her food. It might be a novelty for Joe now, but after over 20 years of taking note of her quirky foods, I was glad I only had to put up with it once a week now.

"Well done, Joseph."

On Mother's plummy tongue, his name came out as Jo-zeff: she did not call him Joe.

I poked at my crumbed lamb chop. Yep, so many ways to make the classic Aussie weeknight dinner fancier. Just go with the dried tarragon.

"So, I hear you've made some progress with the wedding planning?" Joe started his probing.

Mother picked up her wine glass, holding it with her pinky finger outstretched as she took a delicate sip.

"Oh, yes, but we still have so much to do."

I took a deep breath to stop myself from downing my wine.

"Surely we can bring in a wedding planner for that, though? It must be taking up so much of your time..."

Mother sniffed. "Yes, well, the ones I spoke to had *some* experience with these matters, but they had such different ideas."

69

Yes, simple ones. Ones I liked.

I hacked into my lamb chop with more force than was necessary, given that I was using a very sharp steak knife that I was not thinking about using for violent purposes, no, not all.

"It is, it is, but I truly don't mind."

"A guy I worked with was married recently, and he said that they used a website that lets you plan the wedding palette. A heap of companies have joined, and you can do a virtual ceremony and reception mock-up."

Bless the man. He had come prepared.

"Yeah, Joe was showing me." I took up the story. "They had a heap of those napkin designs you were looking at last night, Mum. We can set it up with actual suppliers, and then they can place bids for the work. It's like a formal contract thing."

"What, like eBay for weddings?" She looked honestly appalled.

I held in a snigger with heroic effort.

Almost like he sensed my disrespectful reaction, Dad looked up from his plate and caught my eyes. My not-snigger died in the face of his disappointment.

"No, not quite like eBay," Joe said. "It's more about being able to put together all of your choices and see how they would look. You can choose your colour palette for the bridesmaids and put everything together, from the invitations to the thank you cards."

A huge smile broke out on Mum's face. A wave of relief rushed over me.

"Oh, Lucy, he knows about thank you cards. You didn't even know about the need for thank you cards!"

Brilliant, maybe she'd ask him to help plan the rest of the wedding.

He reached for my hand and gave it a quick squeeze.

"So, what do you think, Mum? Shall we have a look at the website after dinner?" I asked.

"Oh goodness, how could you simply make decisions

from a *screen* for your wedding. No, no. We simply cannot."

"Dad, what do you think? Is Mum getting stressed out about the wedding?"

Dad looked up from his plate. "Hmm?"

Bless him, I think he'd given up trying to take part in a conversation that included Mother before I was born.

"Do you think the wedding planning is stressing Mum out? Taking up too much of her time?"

I held my breath, hoping that he would somehow know what I needed the answer to be.

"Oh, no, I shouldn't think so. It's been giving her something to talk to the ladies at bridge and tea about, hasn't it?"

And wasn't that the point.

"Oh yes, indeed it has." Mother said. "And just imagine what they'll all think when I mention an internet service, my goodness!"

I held in my groan and breathed in and out slowly. I had a feeling that I was going to start getting heartburn from the tarragon potatoes, which also tasted like they contained more garlic than potato.

"Speaking of napkins, dear, we really must get together next Wednesday to discuss your options. We have to make these decisions quickly. We might have to order custom-made ones if the ones we want aren't available to hire."

My jaw dropped momentarily.

"Napkins? Like, printed paper and throw it in the bin?" I asked.

"Oh goodness, no! Not serviettes! Linen napkins. Sherryn down the street had custom napkins *and* tablecloths for her wedding."

Sherryn down the street married a legitimate millionaire and had celebrities and paparazzi at her wedding. She could justify customised linens.

"Now, I'm not saying we should go that far, but I do want you to go through the catalogues with me."

My eyes scrunched with confusion. "Why do we need to

buy napkins for sixty people? It seems a little extreme."

"Sixty people?" Mother said. "That can't be all the people you're inviting, surely? Oh dear, perhaps we should have spoken about the guest list earlier."

Joe must have sensed my blood pressure rising. He grabbed my hand and kept squeezing. I turned to look at him. It seemed as though he was squeezing in support rather than irritation, thankfully.

"You're right, Mother. We definitely need to talk more about the wedding."

"Oh yes, I am so looking forward to spending time with you too. A little treat before you fly the coop."

"Mother, I've been living on my own for two and a half years."

"Oh yes, but you'll be *married*. It's completely different."

I shook my head to rid it of whatever that was.

"What if we look through them at Lucy's house and write a short-list? Then you can work out the best stylistic choices."

Bless him.

"Oh nonsense, Joseph, you have quite enough to do as it is. Lucy and I can get through it just fine, can't we? I'll just need to have her help me on Wednesdays for the next few months while we get through it all."

Months!

"But she can't." Joe said, "Lucy's in the soup kitchen on Wednesday. They need her help."

"I'm sure they will do just fine without her, just as they have been."

Except they hadn't been. Leila told me she had been working double duties and finishing almost an hour later in the last few weeks.

I followed up this explanation to Mother with: "and you know she's hoping to get pregnant soon. This won't help her chances at all."

"That is her responsibility. Your responsibility is to this wedding. If she gets pregnant and the work is too much for her, she can leave too. That is her prerogative as a volunteer.

"It simply cannot be done any other way. We must meet on Wednesday evenings. You will just have to accept that that is what we have to do to get this wedding organised for you, Lucy. I don't understand why you have been so resistant about this."

I took a deep breath in and somehow managed not to exhale it as a sigh.

"Because I enjoy volunteering at the soup kitchen, Mother. I like being able to put a smile on people's faces, and I like seeing people come back every week. I like to see them go from not trusting me to letting me sit down and give them some positive human interaction."

"Well, I will have to say that I just don't understand it. But we all have to make sacrifices at different times of our lives..."

Joe squeezed my hand. "You're right. We will both have to make sacrifices at different stages. Why don't we both come on a Wednesday together?"

I held in my growl. She drove me crazy, but she was my mother. The only one I had. I didn't want to upset or disappoint her.

I caved.

February 14, 12:05 p.m.
Searching for sandwiches

The street was weirdly quiet as I walked towards the supermarket.

The few people on the street were shuffling almost aimlessly. Some were even meandering across the road, which was empty of cars, fortunately. I thought I caught a few odd glances in my direction, not surprising since it was midday, and I was parading myself down the street in a wedding gown.

I mostly ignored them.

I did make an exception for the group of teenage boys who wolf-whistled and called out to ask where the party was and why they weren't invited. I flipped them the bird.

I stretched my wrist out to ease where the strap of my small clutch rubbed against my skin. Damn I wish this dress had pockets.

I struggled to remember why I had even brought the clutch. My phone!

I fumbled with the clasp as I tried to hold my bouquet and the purse in the same hand. Finally, the phone was in my hand, and I thumbed the screen to get in.

Two missed calls.

Joe.

"Lucy, hi. Sorry, I know I shouldn't be calling you. I just wanted to make sure you were okay. I've been watching the news, and some strange stuff is happening...I'm not sure what it's all about. Can you call me? Thanks, bye. See you soon."

The second call was from Mum.

"Lucy, darling, just letting you know that we've stopped at home for a little longer than we meant to. Your father is just feeling a little queer, so we stopped for some antacids. You know how he gets indigestion when he's excited. Anyway, we might be about fifteen minutes late for the photos in the cottage garden, but never mind, just tell the photographer to go ahead and do the bridesmaids' photos first. Too-rah."

Hah! They won't be too long taking bridesmaid photos. There's only one left!

I clicked through my phone and called Joe.

The call didn't connect.

I mentally scanned through his itinerary for the day. He and the other groomsmen should be heading to the church for their pre-wedding photos.

I swore at the patchy phone coverage. Who knew when I'd be able to get through?

I tried Mum next.

The phone rang out. Knowing her, she was in the middle of a conversation with Dad and wouldn't interrupt it to talk on the phone. Even though it was my wedding day.

I poked my phone back in the clutch with just as much awkwardness as I'd pulled it out.

Finally, I made it to the supermarket.

While the temperature outside was only in the mid-twenties, the short walk at a quick clip still led to some slight glistening on my forehead, and the cool air that engulfed me when the supermarket doors opened was refreshing.

Bridget should have already been out on the street by the time I reached the supermarket. While I was thankful for the brief reprieve from the air conditioning, I was still conscious of my timeline.

I growled under my breath and navigated my skirts through the narrow gates, almost getting wedged when the first one tried to close on me.

I click-clacked through the supermarket, down the blessedly cool aisle with the open dairy and meat cabinets, to the deli section at the rear.

There were three staff members behind the counter. One was at the entrance to the cool room, hands to his mouth and apparently eating something, his bites punctuated with loud, crunching noises. Another had her head in the fish cabinet, her face was covered in green flecks and white goo, and she was devouring a piece of salmon in the window.

"Well, that is definitely not sanitary," I said absently.

She looked up when I spoke and bared her teeth at me, a hunk of meat clenched between her teeth. My stomach lurched.

The third deli staff member was staring at her colleagues, horrified. She had plastered herself against the back wall, squashed between the chicken rotisserie oven and the bench holding the slicing machines.

"Excuse me? Have you seen a lady in a bridesmaid's dress? She was meant to be picking up a platter of sandwiches."

The woman didn't acknowledge me. Just kept flicking her gaze between the woman in the fish freezer and the man in the cool room doorway.

He seemed to hear me because he turned, revealing that his food of choice was a whole chicken carcass.

That was one less for the rotisserie.

I shook my head. That wasn't my concern.

I needed to find my wayward bridesmaid and get out of there.

As if my thoughts had drawn her to me, a rustle of silk came from my right, and Bridget was standing before me.

"Lucy! What are you doing in here?" Bridget asked.

"I came to find you. Something happened to the other three. I think Perry spiked their Champagne. They passed out and attacked the limo driver. We need to find another way to get to the church."

Bridget's face fell. I thought I saw tears gathering in her eyes.

"Oh no! Don't cry, you'll ruin your make-up. Why are you crying?"

"Luce, can't you see what's happened? What's happen*ing*?" She gestured wildly around us.

I scanned our surroundings; I could only see the two crazies and the scared woman behind the deli counter. The man seemed to be lurching towards us now, which was creepy, but the only other unusual thing was that a display of tinned tomatoes had been knocked over, leaving a remarkable trip hazard that a staff member should have already been cleaning up.

"Apart from the supermarket apparently being understaffed today?" I asked.

"Lucy!" Bridget grabbed my face and turned me to look at the man behind the counter. "They're zombies!"

"What?"

I stared at the man who had made it to the deli counter and had his arms outstretched towards us. Raw meat adorned his knuckles, and there were bits of bone in his beard. His eyes were bloodshot, but not just bloodshot. The whites of his eyes were completely red. His face was warped into a snarl.

"Zom-bies." Bridget said the word slowly.

I was a child being taught that the colour of the sky was blue.

"I don't know how or why, but they are quite clearly zombies. The undead. The eaters of flesh and destroyers of the living," Bridget said.

I felt a little dizzy spell run through my body as I lodged this piece of information in with the happenings in the car.

"The others," I said.

A chill wave ran through my body, followed quickly by a hot wave that settled in the pit of my abdomen, pushing bile towards my throat.

"What?" Bridget shout-whispered and grabbed my arm.

"Oh, the others. Perry, Kendall, Nora." The bile threatened to rise higher, and my arms and legs felt hollow. I leaned against the end of an aisle of shelves to hold myself up. "That's what happened to them. It must be a virus or something. Oh God!"

Bridget swayed and looked like she would faint. I grabbed her arms and steadied her.

"I'm not above slapping you to keep you conscious. There are more photos to be taken, but I'm pretty sure the mark will wear off by then."

She shook her head, dipped a perfectly filled and shaped eyebrow at me and cocked her chin.

"Huh?"

"Well, I don't know if you've looked at me in the last few minutes, but I'm still wearing over $6000 in bridal wear, not to mention my lingerie. It's my wedding today, and I need to get to the church to see if my almost-husband is still among the living!"

She looked at me like I was mad, and maybe I was, but really. I was only planning to have one wedding day in my entire life. The outlay on my attire was only the icing on the wedding cake. The photographer and videographer cost almost as much, and let's not even get started on the marquee hire. And then there was the sizable donation my parents had made to repair the church and tidy the gardens.

"Seriously?" She asked.

"Yes! Do you want to be the bridesmaid who gave up on the bride or the bridesmaid who shepherded her bride through a town full of the undead to get her to the church on time?"

I'd placed my hands on her shoulders and was shaking her gently by the end of my pep talk. My bouquet was caught in her hair, and my wristlet slapped against her chest.

She shrugged and gave me a small smile. "Okay. What about the others, though? Shouldn't you postpone because of their deaths? Don't you care?"

Not really. They were never my first choices anyway.

My thoughts briefly went to Leila, and there was a real pang in my stomach. I hoped she was safe.

"Of course, I care," I said, "but they aren't going to be the only people affected by this...thing. There will be a lot of people to mourn, but everyone loves the story of the phoenix rising from the ashes. We are the phoenix!"

"The phoenix?"

"The phoenix!" I shouted, then slapped a hand over my mouth, remembering that there were probably zombies out looking for fresh blood. I repeated the phrase in a whisper.

I turned towards the nearest aisle, made sure it was clear and led the way with a whisper.

"Let's get out of here."

March 27, last year
Volunteer of the year, not

"Lucy. It's so good to hear from you. We've missed your lovely smiling face the last few weeks."

Jeez, Vanessa, way to make me feel like I've put my feet in a pot of hot water and turned it on to boil.

"I know. Leila has been keeping me updated. It seems to have been quite busy in the last few weeks."

"Mmmhmm." I could imagine her bobbing her head in her little nod.

I cringed, swallowed down my anxiety-induced reflux and spoke in a rush.

"Oh my God, Vanessa, I am so sorry, I know you guys have been crazy busy lately, and it isn't going to get any easier with the winter weather moving in, but my mum is really insistent that she will still need me for wedding planning stuff every Wednesday for the foreseeable and I won't be able to come in, and I am so, so sorry to let you down."

Surprisingly, Vanessa's initial reaction was a chuckle. "Lucy, seriously, will you breathe?"

I did so, taking in a breath that I was sure was audible down the phone line.

"Did I mention I'm sorry?"

"Lucy, honey, this is a volunteer position and people can come and go as their lives change. We appreciate any help that can be given, and if it can be given regularly, then that's all the better, but sometimes circumstances change, and people's ability to commit disappears suddenly."

I realised my fingers were tightly wound in my hair when I felt tightness in my scalp. I lowered my hand to my side as

Vanessa continued.

"It's okay. We all know that you and Joe were engaged a couple of weeks ago. We saw the announcement in the paper."

I worked hard to stop my blood from boiling again. That notice had gone in the paper before we'd had the chance to tell all the people who were important to us, and we'd wanted to tell personally. It went out before we'd had the chance to make our own public announcement. I previously suspected that it had stung Vanessa. My suspicions were now confirmed.

At least I could potentially fix that problem.

"You know we didn't take out that notice, don't you? My mum did, without our permission. We hadn't even had a chance to visit Joe's grandparents before that notice was published."

"Oh." Vanessa's tone was unreadable. "No, I didn't know that."

The second half of the sentence seemed to contain censure, but Vanessa was not the sort of person to comment on other people's family dynamics.

"Well, anyway. We understand that things are probably about to become busy for you, and I was expecting that you might need to take some time away.

"I do really hope you will come back after the wedding, though, Lucy. I enjoy working with you."

"Me too," I said. "I do have some ideas, though. How about I draw you up a social media campaign? We can aim to bring in donations and maybe some new volunteers?"

"Oh, Lucy!" Vanessa said. "Yes, please! I've seen some of the other work you've done. That would be so good for the centre."

Relieved that I would still be able to help, even if I couldn't physically be there at serving time one night every week, I ran through the brief plan I had made after dinner the previous night.

February 14, 12:20 p.m.
Deli section danger zone

"What about her?" Bridget pointed to the terrified woman cowering by the rotisserie.

"What do you mean?" I asked.

"We can't just leave her there."

"Well, I don't see how we can get her out."

Dodging around the end of the cabinets was foolish. I expected the zombie deli man would follow us. The woman herself seemed immobilised with fear. As far as I could see, she would be safe as long as she stayed still and quiet. Once we left, he would probably go back to the chicken carcasses, and she would be able to make her escape.

I said as much to Bridget, but she disagreed.

"He could just as easily sniff her out as go back to the other meat."

I sighed and thought quickly. I'd come down the chiller aisle, past the packaged meat.

"Alright. Go get me some disposable gloves and something I can hit him with if he gets too close."

She opened her mouth, but I spoke before she could. "Go!"

I put my clutch and bouquet down on a stack of cans in front of the chiller before I ran back to the meat section.

Chicken drumsticks, chicken skewers, ah, beef steak, perfect. I picked up a couple of packets of each and headed back to the deli section. I swore when I realised all of the packets of meat were vacuum sealed.

I mentally inventoried the store before remembering where the kitchen utensils were. Aisle 4. I set the meat down on the end of the aisle and turned towards the kitchenware.

Halfway down the aisle was a woman with a trolley. She had put her handbag in the child seat of the trolley while leaving the cross-body strap on her shoulder. She must have succumbed to the zombie illness while shopping and was corralled to the trolley by her own handbag. She moved aimlessly down the aisle, alternately moving forward and back and bumping the trolley or herself against the shelves. Her face was towards me, but she seemed too focused on the issue with her trolley to have noticed me.

The scissors were only a metre further down the aisle from where she bumped back and forward.

I watched her bump a couple of times before I moved.

I ran down the aisle, putting more energy into shifting my voluminous skirts than I normally would. I reached my arms forward as I moved, and, as the zombie woman hit the shelves with the front of her trolley, I hit it with both arms outstretched, spinning it slightly and sending her away.

She only made it 3 shelving bays before the trolley smashed into the shelves, pressing her hard against them as bags of flour thumped down around her. Some of them exploded on impact, clouds of flour billowing up and over the uncaring, undead woman.

My push hadn't sent her far, but it was enough to let me safely review the selection of scissors on offer. The poultry shears looked perfect, and I grabbed them with a cry of triumph. My jubilance was short-lived when I realised that the scissors were held tight to the packet with a zip tie.

"How the heck am I meant to get these out? Super useful, a pack of scissors that requires a pair of scissors to open."

I rolled my eyes and hung the scissors back on the rack.

I scanned the other options. The sharp knives were all in plastic packs that would be more impossible to open than the scissors. The butter knives would be next to useless.

An egg slicer, a pack of potato peelers, a citrus reamer, something else random and kitchen related. Wait a second, potato peelers.

I grabbed a pack and flipped it over. The peelers were

packaged on a cardboard tab and held in place with thick, blue tape. Perfect.

I grabbed a fistful of skirt in each hand, slightly more difficult for the hand holding the peelers, and ran back down the aisle to the deli section.

Bridget appeared at the end of the aisle, a look of worry on her face.

"What were you doing down there? There's one of them."

"I know, don't worry, I got her out of the way. Have you got the gloves?"

She handed me a box of gloves, and I thrust the potato peelers at her. "Thanks. Here, get one of these off for me."

"O-kay," she said.

I donned a pair of gloves and reached for a peeler. I held it like a dagger and stabbed the pointy end of the peeler into the plastic seal of the packets, making a hole big enough for me to poke my finger through and peel back the film.

I reached for a chicken drumstick first. He did seem to already have a taste for raw chicken.

I moved down the cabinet to where the zombie was still idly reaching out, making sure I stayed well outside his reach. I tossed a chicken drumstick at him. It thunked against the top of the cabinet and rolled down the front, hitting the floor with a splat. He seemed to catch a whiff of the chicken, and his movements became more frantic, his chest hit the glass with more urgency.

I tossed another drumstick. This one caught him on the cheek before ricocheting off onto the floor behind him.

"Lucy, look."

I looked at Bridget, then followed the direction of her index finger. The female zombie from the fish cabinet had stood slightly and was trying to manoeuvre out of the fridge.

"Keep an eye on her. If she gets out, follow my lead."

My zombie had turned when the chicken bounced off his cheek and was now scrabbling around on the floor for his prize. I tossed another drumstick a little further away. The single-minded zombie nature had him collect one and then the other.

Next, I reached for a steak. It was a nice scotch fillet steak, and I almost felt bad about the waste. Until I remembered that I was putting it to use to rescue someone. I threw the steak overarm, but it was an unfamiliar projectile and only landed a few feet in front of the zombie rather than the few metres I was aiming for. The zombie rushed towards it.

I moved to my left to throw the next steak, almost tripping over a tin of crushed tomatoes in the process. I swore. Further to my left, the female zombie had managed to free herself and was moving her head slowly from Bridget's white face to the steak the male zombie had started to devour.

"Quick, throw something!" I urged.

I tossed the steak in my hand towards the female zombie and grabbed another from the pack to throw for the male.

By the time I had thrown two more steaks, they were almost where I wanted them.

My final projectiles were the chicken skewers.

I picked one up and held it like a javelin. I was aiming for the open door to the cool room. My first throw missed by 10 centimetres, the skewer stabbing point first against the clean white tiles.

The male zombie still got the hint, though. His attention was drawn back to where he had found such bounty earlier. My second skewer sailed through the door, and he happily followed it.

The female was less obliging.

It took two more steaks to get her close to the door and a pile of skewers thrown by Bridget to get her through.

"Come on!" We urged the cowering woman when the two zombies were out of sight.

She remained frozen on the spot.

"You'll have to go and get her," I told Bridget.

I peeled off my gloves and placed them on the cooler

cabinet.

"Why me?" She asked.

"Really?"

"Right, bride, big dress, got it."

I became aware of irritation on my inner biceps and lifted my left arm. Fine pink lines crisscrossed the tender skin.

"What?" I wondered aloud.

I studied my arms a moment before the shimmer of beads caught my eye. The little bastards adorning my dress had scratched my arms up. It must have been a combination of the frontal assault on trolley woman and the meat projectiles. Damn.

Bridget had made her way to the opening at the end of the deli section and was approaching the chicken roasting cabinet.

"Go carefully. She's probably in shock."

Indeed, the woman seemed immune to all of the action around her, staring almost unblinkingly ahead.

Bridget slowly made her way to the end of the cabinet and poked her head around at the woman. When the woman remained motionless, Bridget tentatively reached out a hand and touched the woman's forearm.

The woman jumped as if electrocuted and screamed loud enough to drown out a fire alarm.

The sound stopped when she drew a breath, but it was only a pause. The sound started again, just as loud as before. Bridget looked at me with fear in her eyes, wordlessly asking me what to do next.

I looked towards the cool room to find the two zombies shuffling out together, momentarily halted in their progress as they wedged each other in place.

"I don't know," I shouted to be heard over the woman. "Slap her?"

Bridget paused only a moment before raising a hand and slapping the woman square across the cheek. Instead of rousing her, the slap seemed to knock her back into a stupor, but at least she stopped screaming.

The vacuum of silence was swiftly filled by shuffling and groaning. To my horror, the sounds weren't emanating solely from the two cool room zombies, it seemed to be coming from every aisle in the supermarket.

"Bridget." My voice rose. "You'd better drag her out here."

She grabbed the woman by the arm. Thankfully, the woman followed the physical prompt and tripped along behind Bridget.

While I waited for them, I ran along the back of the supermarket and checked out the aisles. The situation did not look good.

Each of the first five aisles held at least three zombies making their way towards us at a much greater speed than the deli zombies had led me to believe was the undead norm.

The next aisle held more zombies than I could count at a quick glance, but the seventh seemed to hold only two: one only a few metres away and the other right down the far end near the checkouts, blissfully close to the exit doors.

"Bridget, where's that weapon I asked for?"

"I couldn't find anything," she said, desperation knocking her voice up half an octave.

I cursed.

The end cap to my left held a random assortment of socks, heat packs and other almost-winter gear, but on my right was an assortment of tinned cat food. Perfectly sized 400-gram tins of chicken casserole, sardines in jelly and turkey and cranberry goo projectiles.

I grabbed the closest tin and threw it at the nearest zombie's head. My throw was too high, but the can knocked a few others from the shelf on impact, and one of these hit the zombie in the head, knocking him down.

Bridget was at my side, still holding tight to the still-breathing deli staff member. Now that she was close enough, I could read her name tag—Wendy.

I grabbed a tin of cat food in each hand and led the way down the aisle, not caring when my skirt trailed through the puddle of blood leaking from the head of the zombie but being careful not to step in it in case I slipped.

I threw the first of my tins when I was 3 metres from the next zombie, missing completely. Damn my terrible hand-eye coordination. And damn the beading on the dress, sore arms were not in the advertisement.

A whoosh passed my ear, and I looked up to see a can of dog food land at the zombie's feet.

I turned to glower at Bridget.

"Sorry!"

I turned back and threw my next tin, but that missed too, hitting the ground a metre further back and bouncing the rest of the way down the aisle.

I screeched in frustration.

We were in the pet food aisle, and I started pulling down and throwing can after can of cat food, then dog food. My fury made my aim even worse and can after can missed. The only exception was one that hit the zombie in the shin. The impact would have sent most living humans to their knees, but she felt no pain.

I turned back to look at Bridget for ideas, only to see Wendy running past like a berserker, a bulk bag of dog biscuits held against her chest like a shield as she ran down the aisle, dodged Bridget and me and ploughed into the chest of the nearest zombie.

She pulled her arms free of the bag of biscuits just in time, jamming it between herself and the zombie as they went down. Wendy jumped back up quickly, landing on her feet in a boxer's pose. She placed a foot on the crotch of the floored zombie and kicked out. The zombie slid along the floor about half a metre. Wendy repeated the process again and again until she had the aisle cleared of zombies.

She turned back to Bridget and me, we hadn't moved since she rushed past us.

"Come on!"

Not needing to be told twice, Bridget and I raced down the aisle after her.

I realised as we got to the end of the aisle that I'd left my clutch and my bouquet near the deli cabinets. I looked back down the aisle.

The three zombies Wendy had charged were rising to their feet, and they'd been joined by the two zombies from the deli section.

I wouldn't be going back for my belongings.

We emerged at the front of the supermarket, near the checkouts.

Two of the three checkouts were blocked with trolleys chained across the aisles. The third checkout was open but contained a zombie who was just standing in the aisle.

The self-checkout area looked clear, but foul noises were coming from the area.

We looked over the low wall and between the checkouts when we were close enough. I spied three bodies on the ground. One was prone, and the other two were crouched over it. I pulled back before I saw more than I wanted to.

The last point of possible exit was the entrance.

Unfortunately, the area between the automatic doors and the entrance was slowly filling with zombies whose attention was drawn by the moving doors. As we watched, the doors opened again, and two more zombies stumbled in.

"We're trapped," Bridget whispered.

"This way." Wendy said. "We'll go out the fire exit."

April 11, last year
Expectant

"So, how are the wedding plans going?" Leila asked.

I took a sip of my wine before speaking, swirling it in my mouth and savouring the hint of passionfruit.

"We are...progressing." I hedged my response.

She dipped a corn chip into the salsa and crunched in.

"Go on."

"Do I have to?" I whined. "Mother has just been making all these decisions, and I'm not sure about them, to be honest."

"Tell her no!" Leila half laughed at me.

"I try to!" I said. "Have you ever tried to say no to my mother? She wraps your words around until even you think you've agreed to something and don't realise until later that you didn't after all, but now you have to do it anyway because there is no other way around it."

Leila's eyes were sympathetic as she reached out and patted my leg.

"You'll get there. If all else fails, just elope somewhere and tell her after. Nate can do it."

She sing-songed the last part, and, for a moment, it was a very tempting offer.

I sighed. "Yeah, I probably shouldn't."

She smiled and patted my leg again.

"Ah, here come the fellows to cheer us up."

The scent of beef and barbecue sauce wafted ahead of Joe and Nate as they carried in a plate of baked meatballs and pastry puffs.

"Ah, the gentle men of our lives," I said.

Leila giggled.

"Ladies, your snacks."

Joe placed the platter down on the coffee table with a flourish.

We giggled. Joe sat in the armchair next to me, and Nate joined Leila, grabbing her hand and pulling it into his lap.

"Alright, let's get into these snacks."

Joe rubbed his hands together, waggled his fingers over the plate and finally picked up a meatball between his thumb and forefinger.

Leila's nose wrinkled just slightly, for just a moment.

"About that..." she said.

She and Nate shared a look. It was most definitely a *look*. It carried weight and subtext.

"Yes?" I said, urging her on.

"Well, we have some news to share," Nate said.

"News related to me definitely not wanting to eat certain foods and having to avoid certain drinks," Leila said with a small smile.

Joe looked at me, head cocked to the side in slight bafflement.

"Really?" My voice squeaked.

Leila's smile broadened, and her eyes gleamed.

"Really."

I squealed, completely forgetting about the men in the room as I leaned forward to hug her.

"That is so exciting! Tell me all the details. How far along are you? When are you due? How are you feeling?"

She giggled.

I dimly registered some backslapping and congratulations between the boys, but all my attention was focused on Leila.

"It's only really early yet," Leila said. "I'm about seven weeks along, but I'll be going for a scan next week to check the heartbeat and confirm. I should be due about the seventh of December."

"No-one else knows yet, though. It's just between us," Nate said.

91

"Of course!" I said.

"Yeah, man," Joe said.

Leila and Nate shared a look that conveyed love. Gentle, encompassing, accepting love. And quiet joy. It was beautiful.

I probed her on how she'd been feeling.

"I had the worst stomach-ache a couple of weeks ago. I felt all sorts of nausea and just ick. I think that might have been when it, what's the term? Implanted? Since then, I've been mostly okay. A little bit of nausea in the afternoon if I go too long without a snack, but other than that, pretty good."

"Oh, this is going to be so awesome for you, a Christmas baby. I am so happy for you both," I said.

"Me too." Joe agreed.

"Thank you," Leila said.

February 14, 12:40 p.m.
Unexpected company

Thankfully, the alley was empty.

Aside from the stench of a half-full dumpster in a heatwave. That smell had presence.

Wendy allowed the fire escape doors to close behind us, silencing the screeching alarm.

I rubbed my ears, that thing was shrill, and it echoed.

I studied the unexpectedly dark space. The buildings on either side of the alley were only a single storey high, with roofs peaking in the middle, where they rose almost two storeys. The roof beams extended from one building to the next, and the corrugated iron roofing sheets bridged the 3-metre span from wall to wall. Fluorescent light bulbs in plastic cases dotted the walls on either side of the alley. Despite the smell, there was no dumpster in sight. Although there were plenty of suspicious-looking marks on the wall that sprayed from the average man's crotch height and a couple of suspicious-looking puddles on the ground.

I winced at the unexpected pull of hair over my right ear as I pulled my hand down. I had completely forgotten about the umbrella.

I had spotted the stand of umbrellas as we had run past the checkouts, hooked a long one out of the rack and kept running to the doors.

I released the hooked handle from my hair and studied it. My quick glance had paid off. It was a sturdy little steel umbrella with a nice blue handle and a clear plastic canopy with a white lace print, perfectly appropriate for a bride. The best feature was the pointed silver tip. In the battle to the church, it should serve me well.

Wendy studied the umbrella too.

"Damn, I wish I'd grabbed one of those.

"Thank you for getting me out of there. They went crazy, and I just couldn't think. It was like I was asleep. Things were happening around me, and I couldn't do anything to stop it."

"You're welcome," I said, speaking for Bridget too.

Bridget had burst out of the fire doors and was crouched down on the opposite side of the alley, her head bowed forward over her hands, her bottom against the wall to steady herself.

"Bridge?" I called softly from my spot a metre away. "Are you okay?"

Her chest heaved, and I braced myself as she lifted her head, but only tears were in her eyes.

"They're all dead? Perry, Kendall, Nora?"

I nodded slowly.

"Who else? Your parents? My parents? Our friends?"

A shudder ran down my body, and goosebumps rose on my arms.

"What's the time?" I asked.

Bridget squinted her eyes at me. "Why?"

I scrambled to find an answer to the question other than: because I'm still wearing a $6000 dress and $2000 shoes, and I intend to get married, dammit.

"Because at three o'clock, many of the people we know and love will be St Columba's Church, waiting to see me walk down the aisle. Given how Perry and Kendall were acting, some may feel a bit like they have the flu and might try to get to the ceremony anyway, which means they could turn into zombies at any minute and attack.

"We still need to get to the church, and while we're at it, we may as well get me married."

"Twelve forty-five," Wendy said from behind me. "Good luck with that. I'm off home to barricade the doors with my husband and children. Actually, I might barricade them in the house and myself in the granny flat."

She studied the detritus around the dumpster and

kicked a few things with her foot. She leaned down and picked up a rough timber two-by-four that looked to have broken off a nearby pallet.

"Can I give you two a ride anywhere? I probably won't take you to the church, but I might be able to drop you at one of your houses. Maybe the bridesmaid's, not sure you'd fit in behind the wheel."

I looked at Bridget. She was slowly rising from her crouch.

"My place is only a few streets away," she said. "We should be able to walk it."

"Really? In spike heels?" I asked.

She smiled. "Toughen up, Princess. You can do this."

"If you say so." I turned to Wendy; she was already halfway down the alley to the rear car park. "Thanks for the offer. Good luck!"

She threw her hand up in a wave without turning back to us and disappeared around the corner.

"Which way to yours?" I turned to find Bridget halfway down the alley in the opposite direction and picked up my skirt so I could run behind her.

I swore at the skirts.

"Wait," I said. "Can you tuck the damn train up on this dress before we go? The dragging is driving me crazy."

Bridget came back down the alley, and I turned, my train twirling around my feet in the collection of dirt and rubbish. I wrinkled my nose, my poor dress.

"How do I even do this? Nora was the one who learnt how to do the bustle."

"There's a little loop on the train, tucked into the lace about where it hits the ground. It goes over the little clear button at the bottom of the lacing on my back."

Bridget squatted down again and scoured the twisted pile of lace. "Where?"

"Hang on, let me walk straight a bit. It might need to straighten out."

I winced at the dirt that would be collecting on the thick

satin lining and walked 3 metres down the alley to give it plenty of space to flatten out.

"Hang on, go a little further, so you're under the next light."

Bridget duck walked over and finally shouted in victory.

I felt a tug and pull on the back of the skirt and a redistribution of weight. A noise at the far end of the alley made me turn from watching Bridget work at my derriere.

A zombie had just appeared at the mouth of the alley. As I watched, two more appeared.

"How are you going there, Bridget?" I tried to keep my voice as calm as possible. I didn't want her to get nervous and have more trouble with the tiny button.

"Almost done. Although, that doesn't quite look right," she mused. "I wonder if there was a second loop..."

I sensed her stand, and she moved back a step to survey her work.

"It's still on the ground by about a foot and...oh yes, there is a second loop, let me just..."

The first zombie was lurching nearer with slow, steady, inexorable progress. His arms were still by his side, but the third zombie was moving slightly faster and already had her hands outstretched.

"Almost done?" A little bit of terror must have entered my voice, and I felt Bridget freeze.

"Why?" Her voice sounded husky.

"Just, we've got a little company coming. Probably heard the alarm."

Her head appeared in my peripheral vision, at hip height, peering around my waist. She drew a sharp breath in.

"Ok." The was a grinding of dirt as she pivoted around. "We do have a couple coming from the way Wendy went too. Hopefully, she made it out okay."

"Mmmhmmm. So, how is that skirt coming along? Do you think I'll be able to run a bit faster in it yet?"

"I think it's time we found out," Bridget said, standing.

"Which way?"

I looked to the street end of the alley. Half a dozen zombies were scattered across the wide alley, the closest one about 4 metres away and the furthest just at the entrance of the alley, 6 metres or so from where we stood. In the other direction, where Wendy had disappeared, we had further to travel before we were out in the open, about 10 metres, but there were only four zombies, although one more appeared as I watched.

"That way," I said, hoping I sounded more confident than I felt.

April 22, last year
Napkins and bridesmaids

"Very good," Mother said. "That is another decision made."

About napkins. Finally.

I had already approved five different designs, but apparently, my decisions had been wrong, even though I had just been trying to agree with Mother's suggestions.

First, the apricot ones had been too close to peach. Then the jacquard ones were debossed too deeply. I hadn't even known the words jacquard and debossed 3 weeks ago, but here we were.

She wrote the name of the design and supplier in the little white wedding book she had bought when we announced our engagement. The pages were starting to fill with the details she was cataloguing for the day.

"The next decision we need to make will be about the colour of the bridesmaids' dresses." Mother said.

"Can we even decide that now? Don't we need to choose my dress first to make sure the bridesmaids match?" I asked.

I took a pickled onion and cheese toothpick off the little plate of snacks she had prepared and slid the food into my mouth.

"Your dress will be white."

Her voice had a note of steel that I had learnt was her absolutely telling me how things would happen.

I reminded myself that I was an adult and trying to stand up for myself.

"Well, it doesn't have to be, though, does it? There are some lovely cream and champagne colours to choose from.

Or I could choose a gown with coloured accents. I saw one with a painted design online the other day. Any of those might just be perfect."

Mother placed her pen down carefully, lining it up perfectly with the margin of her notebook.

"Lucy," she said. "You will be wearing white.

"Pure white. There will be no coloured beading or—" she gave a delicate shudder, "—painting on your gown. White and white alone."

I held in a swear word.

"Well, why don't we wait until we go dress shopping? Let's keep our minds open. We might come across something that is just right. I really did love the dress my friend Frieda had last year. Do you remember? It had red around the bodice and then inset in the train."

"Red! Red is simply not done for a wedding, Lucy. A bride should be demure and reserved. Not red."

"Actually, Chinese bridal gowns are red. The colour symbolises good luck and happiness. And did you know that in ancient Rome, they wore yellow dresses? And in Athens, they wore violet or reddish robes?"

"Lucy, do we live in China, Rome or Athens?"

My heart sank a little. "No."

"No, we do not. We live in Sky Valley, where brides wear white."

My heart sank further. It wasn't like I actually wanted to wear a red wedding dress. I just wanted to make a clear decision of my own about something to do with my wedding. I sighed.

"Okay. Luckily, the wedding boutiques in town tend to stock a lot of white dresses, so we should be able to find one that suits."

My tone must have carried some of my displeasure.

"Enough, Lucy. You know I only have your best interests at heart. What if you wear a purple dress and regret the decision when you look back at the photos? You want classic, my dear. Then your photos will be elegant enough for your grandchildren to be impressed."

Lord, those grandchildren would have a lot to answer for when they arrived, that was for sure.

"Yes, yes. What do we need to look at next? I can probably think about one more thing tonight, and then I have to go home. It has been a busy week."

"Well, we must discuss the bridesmaids." Mother said.

My heart squeezed at this one. I knew this topic would be difficult.

"Well, we will start with Leila as matron of honour, of course."

"Ah yes, how is she? Are they doing well? Have they announced their pregnancy yet?"

I was shocked. How on earth would Mother have found out?

"Ah, I can see by your face that I was right!" She crowed. "I just knew she was pregnant at your engagement party. I can tell these things."

"What?" I said.

"Lucy. Manners."

"Sorry, Mum. What do you mean, you knew? She didn't even know. I don't think she could have even *been* pregnant then. She's only nine weeks now, and the engagement party was nine weeks ago."

She pounced on the information. "I knew I could get it out of you."

I felt like a bucket of ice water had been poured over my head.

"Mum, honestly, you can't tell anyone. No-one else even knows yet apart from Joe and me, as far as I know. You cannot breathe a word of this to anyone."

She gave a toad-like smile. "The secret is safe with me but do let's think about whether we include her in the wedding now.

"When will she be due? Did she tell you?"

"Early December."

She nodded. "Right, and the wedding is the fourteenth

of February, so the baby could be anywhere from, well, if she's overdue, it could be less than two months to three months old. That's quite young. Leila may have only just recovered from the birth."

"I'm sure she will still want to be involved in the wedding, Mother. And Nate too. We can have the baby as a mini-flower girl or page boy. We will be able to work it out."

"Well, if you think it is really fair on her. I know that I never would have wanted to think about making sure that I would fit in my bridesmaid dress or be able to stay awake through the whole process of preparing for a wedding ceremony when you were that small. Why I could barely get myself out of bed some days."

That, I found hard to believe.

"Well, we can always talk about that later, and both she and Nate can pull out if they feel the need to.

"But it would be so unfair of you to make them feel like they are letting you down." She put a little pout on her face.

Again, I felt there was no way she would accept any answer but the one she wanted.

"Look, I'll talk to Joe about it, and we'll think about it. But it is our wedding, Mother. We have to make some of the decisions ourselves."

February 14, 12:50 p.m.
Battle in the alley

Bridget surveyed the broken pallet near the dumpster, braced her foot against the bottom and hauled at a plank. The piece of timber was only held in with two nails at the top, and she levered it upward, releasing the timber from the frame.

"Ouch." She said, shaking her hand as the timber tore free.

"Are you okay? I asked.

"Splinter."

I looked at the rough piece of timber she was gripping, glanced at the incoming five zombies and decided there wasn't time to fix that problem just yet.

"Wait." I groped around in the bodice of my dress and produced two latex gloves. "Here, I stashed a couple more of these in case I needed them."

She nodded her thanks, pulled the gloves on and reclaimed her piece of timber.

"We'll look at the splinter later."

We approached the first zombie cautiously, unsure of how she would react to our presence. She was shuffling along in roughly the middle of the alley. Her knees seemed fused, and she moved forward by rising up on one side and arcing the other leg out and around to the side. Her shoulders were pulled in towards each other, her hands in tight claws, tyrannosaurus-like, in front of her. She wore running shorts and shoes with a sports bra, and her activity tracker watch flashed a red warning light. I knew that some tracked heart rates and could warn of medical emergencies. This lady was beyond the help of emergency services.

I looked at her face last.

Her hair appeared to have been in a neat ponytail when she had started her exercise, but the tie had slipped loose, and the ponytail sagged. Hanks of hair had been pulled loose, and dirt, blood and something I didn't want to try to identify adorned the style.

"You go that way," I whispered.

Bridget nodded and skirted the zombie on the left while I hugged the right-hand side of the alley. The back of my skirt pressed against the wall, and the front billowed out. I tried to flatten it with the umbrella, so I didn't bump the zombie.

The runner zombie lurched on slowly, not seeming to notice as we crab-walked the alley on either side of her.

A clang echoed through the alley. I almost jumped out of my Louboutin's.

My eyes shot straight to Bridget's. Her eyes were wide saucers of horror.

She had knocked over a length of unpainted steel roof guttering that had been leaning against the wall. The base of the guttering was between her feet, and the other end had fallen towards the opening of the alley.

The runner zombie turned her head slowly towards the noise...and Bridget.

Bridget was frozen against the wall, within lurching reach of the Zombie, whom I was within lunging reach of.

"Bridget," I whispered as loudly as I dared, "go back that way, then come around past her on this side. Kick the gutter away if you can."

She didn't answer, just looked down briefly, kicked the gutter towards the edge of the alley, making a shrill scrape that caught runner zombie's attention, and ducked back to my left.

Once Bridget was out of range, I lunged forward with the tip of my umbrella, aiming for the base of runner zombie's skull.

It wasn't sharp enough, or I wasn't fierce enough, to pierce her skin, but it did send her off balance, and her slowed responses did not save her from falling on her face. She sprawled down, and Bridget appeared beside me.

"One down." She said.

"Three to go—oh."

My jubilation was short-lived.

A tight knot of bodies had edged around the corner of the alley while we were distracted by runner zombie. The original three were still in the lead, but I estimated another dozen were behind them.

I swore and turned back the other way.

The six there had been joined by others too, but the ten before us were outnumbered by the fifteen behind us.

"What do we do?" Bridget said.

I bit the inside of my lip.

"Umm."

I studied the walls of the alley, checking for any other exits.

The only doors were the firmly closed fire doors of the supermarket. What I wouldn't do for one of Batman's shooty grappling hook thingies to get me out of this.

"I guess we have to go back that way, but this time, just run."

She nodded, and we took our first running steps back down the alley, the click of our heels a sharp counterpoint to the shuffling susurrus of the zombies.

I dodged a man who may have been in his eighties on my right and a teenage girl on my left. My skirt tangled in the latter's legs and brought her down, almost toppling me with her. I yanked on my remaining train just as she would have pinned it, dragging the crisp, white fabric across her blood-stained face.

Ignoring the plight of my attire, I turned my eyes forward again to see a zombie closing in. I swung my umbrella up and whacked the zombie in the face before I even got a good look at it. It reeled backward and took down two others, domino-style.

I took the moment's reprieve to look over at Bridget. Her

piece of pallet was heading in a fierce upswing and caught a zombie in the chin. His teeth clacked together, and blood sprayed from his mouth into her face. She grimaced and stepped around the body as it fell.

I looked back to my own path. I estimated 4 more metres to the end of the alley.

I could do it.

Bridget could do it.

We would survive this alley of bloodshed.

There was a zombie to my left, and I charged at him. Some sense of self-preservation must have remained because the zombie took a step backward and bumped into another body behind him.

Only three more zombies and three more metres.

As before, just as freedom seemed possible, a phalanx of zombies appeared, four on either side of the alley. They were a metre beyond where the end of the alley but would move much closer in the moments it would take us to reach them.

Bridget swore loudly.

My heart became a stone in my chest.

Our window of opportunity for escape had closed.

April 26, last year
Shades of cream

Joe, bless him, rubbed my feet, which were crossed at the ankles and in his lap. I was flopped with my shoulders over the back of the couch, moaning about Mother.

"She's a monster!" I said. "I don't understand how there are so many different shades of cream to choose from for invitation card stock."

Joe picked up my left foot and rubbed his thumbs firmly into the arch of my foot. I moaned for a completely different reason this time.

"I don't know how to help with this," Joe said.

I sighed.

"No. I know. I don't know what to do about it either."

I reached over to the table to pick up a corn chip, crunching it as I pondered further on which points of the most recent debacle of a planning session needed to be discussed.

"There is also the matter of the bridal party."

"What about it?" Joe asked.

I picked at a loose thread on the blanket across my lap and sighed again.

"Well, I wanted to have Leila, and you wanted to have Nate, right? Was there anyone else you wanted?"

"Yeah, of course, we want Leila and Nate. Then I will have my two younger brothers and my mate Greg from high school."

"Oh yeah, it will be great to meet him! And to get your brothers in town, they were great fun at Christmas.

"I think they will be a great group for you."

He smiled and switched to massaging my right foot.

"Me too."

"Mum isn't sure about Leila and Nate, though."

He stopped rubbing and locked eyes with me.

"Why?"

"Well, I guess it's because of the baby. Mother believes that Leila and Nate will be too tired for the wedding and feels like it's too much pressure on them or something."

"What do you think?"

"I don't know," I said. "It was a lot of work as Leila's maid of honour last year. I did a heap of prep work. I helped pick and pack bonbonniere and place cards and all sorts of stuff in the week before the wedding. I had to take a week off work."

Nate cocked his head at me.

"You chose to take the week off work because you were so excited about helping out. You didn't have to. I'm sure that Leila and Nate would have managed without you."

"Maybe," I said, although I wasn't convinced.

"There's the hen's party and all that stuff to organise too."

"You can always delegate that to your other bridesmaids. Who else are you having?"

"I'm not sure yet. I think my cousin Kendall? I don't know who else. I don't really have any other close friends, and I've known Leila forever. Mum will probably suggest a few people, I guess."

The loose thread was now long enough to wrap around my finger three times, and I tugged it again to make the thread even longer.

"Where will she get her suggestions from?" Joe asked.

"Oh, I'm sure her Club ladies will be able to suggest appropriate bridesmaids. Ugh, I just don't know."

He patted my leg and reached for the hand that was worrying at the blanket.

"You don't have to solve all of your problems at once. We can work through them one at a time. Did you manage to choose a shade of cream for the invitations?"

I groaned, grunted my way upright and moved to where I had left an envelope of samples Mother had given me a few days earlier.

"Okay, let's see, I have six shades."

I fanned out the 5 × 5 cm squares of cardstock.

They were named Parchment, Ivory, Oxford Cream, Smooth Cream, Speckletone Cream and just plain Cream.

"I...I can't see a difference."

Joe took the pieces of card from my hand and held them under the lamp.

"Nope. No difference, oh...except...I think I can make out a speckle in this one." He flipped the sample over and read the name. "Speckletone Cream."

I laughed.

"Shall we choose that one then, since it clearly stands out from the others?"

"Yes, it is a clear winner," Joe said, sombrely but with a smile big enough to give a lie to his tone.

I pulled a pillow from behind me and smacked him with it.

"You are terrible. I bet I could shuffle those, and you wouldn't be able to pick it out a second time."

"I bet I could," he said. "Go on."

I did as threatened and shuffled the card samples.

As predicted, he could not repeat the performance and chose the Oxford Cream instead of the speckle.

"Ha! I told you!"

He grabbed the cushion I had previously used as a weapon and tossed it at me. He followed up the cushion by grabbing my hands with his and pulling me to him for a kiss.

"You know I don't care about the fluff, right?"

I sighed again, relaxing into him as I rested my forehead against his.

"I know. I love you."

"You too," he said before he kissed me again.

February 14, 1:00 p.m.
Unexpected quarters

"Lucy?" Bridget called, panicked.

I looked at her. She was almost pressed against the wall opposite me. Three zombies were closing in on her.

I swore. My umbrella was not going to get through that lot.

"Where's your plank?"

She pointed to the ground. It was closer to me than her.

I dropped my umbrella and picked up the rough plank. I gripped it with a hand on either side of the plank and hit the zombie on her left.

I was aiming for his ear, but my aim was off, and I cracked him on the temple. He crumpled forward, almost pinning Bridget against the wall.

She shrieked.

I ignored her and moved on to the next zombie. I dropped the plank, hefted up my skirts and kicked him firmly in the crotch. He toppled away, and I danced back.

I bumped into another body behind me and shrieked. Without thinking, I formed a fist with my right hand and swung my whole body to thwack the body in the jaw. I made the error of assuming the jaw would be at my height, but it was a young boy, a half-head shorter than where I was aiming.

I let the momentum of my punch keep turning my body and aimed my hip out, so I caught the boy with a glancing blow that sent him spinning away from me.

I picked up the piece of timber and wielded it at Bridget's last attacker. Except Bridget had quite capably floored him herself while I was distracted.

"Nice one," I said.

"You too." She agreed.

"Keep fighting?" I asked.

"For sure."

I retrieved my umbrella, wondering if I would be able to poke it hard enough at someone when the need arose, or maybe it would serve like a traditional Japanese sword to fall upon instead.

Just as I was contemplating the act of self-euthanasia on my wedding day, my musings were interrupted by beeping.

I looked towards the other end of the alley to see the sea of zombies being parted by a hot pink Nissan Micra.

The tiny car continued beeping as it ten-pin bowled the zombies down the alley, headlights and wipers on as it careened towards us.

"Who...?" I asked.

"It's Wendy!" Bridget said.

She ran across the alley before the car arrived with a screeching of brakes and pulled up next to us.

"Get in," Wendy shouted.

Her prompt was unneeded. I already had the back door open.

My upper body bent in through the tiny opening easily, but I was halted by the skirts. Again.

"Whose damned idea was a three-metre-long train?!"

I heard the other car door slam as Bridget got in the front seat.

"I don't know," Wendy said, "but if you aren't all in, you'd better hold on tight!"

She slammed the car into first gear, dropped the clutch and sped out of the alley like a cork. I just managed to get the majority of my body into the car and get a grip on the driver's seat before she gunned it towards the collection of zombies coming towards us.

The open door jolted, thumping my shins as it was pushed in by the passing undead bodies.

I bumped up in the seat as we passed over a speed bump—yes, a speed bump, there must have been a speed bump, only thing it could have been—and my head bumped against the low roof of the tiny car. It would have hurt if it weren't for my stylish updo.

I held on for dear life as Wendy swerved the car violently left when she hit the main street. My own momentum nearly pulled me out of the still-open right-hand door.

"Slow down!" I shrieked.

"I can't!"

My head was pointing down to the ground as I gripped.

"Of course, you can!"

"No, she really can't," Bridget said.

I lifted my head up and peered between the two headrests. The street was scattered with zombies.

My arms were screaming with the effort of gripping the car seat. My left leg was braced against the lip of the doorframe inside the car and starting to cramp. My right leg was trying to work out a way of supporting me too, but there was nowhere for it to brace against.

"Alright," I said. "Just lay off the accelerator for a minute."

The car slowed down just a little, and I whispered a quick prayer before letting go of the car seat.

I turned and hauled my skirts into the car with as much strength as I could muster. The tight springs of the hoop skirt put up resistance as I hauled them through the door, and then they sprang open again, flashing my bridal underwear to the—thankfully empty–street.

My torso was flung backward as the springs sprung, and I lay dazed across the back seat of the car.

"I think she's all in," Bridget said. "Gun it again."

The car took off again at great speed. A short gust of wind fanned across my inner thighs before it managed to slam the car door closed. I was now well and truly wedged in the back seat, my bodice sliding down my torso, my skirts around my knees, and a madwoman driving me around my hometown.

I feared this would be a highlight of the day.

April 30, last year
Horseradish

"This is a lovely dinner. What have you added to the mashed potato tonight?" Joe asked.

I held back a snigger with a great force of will. Joe and I had mercilessly grilled Mother's potatoes with tarragon after the family dinner a few weeks earlier.

"Thank you, Joseph, dear. I've added horseradish to the potatoes tonight. Doesn't it just bring out the lemon pepper in the schnitzel crumb?"

"Oh, yes, I find horseradish always goes well with crumbed chicken."

Dad nodded and hummed his agreement.

"Lucy?" Mother asked, seeming to wait for my praise of the meal.

"Oh yes," I said, "and the boiled broccoli just really sets it off."

She gave me a look that suggested she didn't quite take my compliment at face value; it was fair, given how I'd described her dinners in the past.

"Ah," Joe said, saving me from further scrutiny. "Did Lucy tell you last night that we chose the cardstock for our invitations?"

I winced. I had not had a chance to tell Joe how that conversation had panned out.

Mother pulled her lips together in a tight moue. "Oh, yes, she did tell me you'd discussed it."

"Ah, good," he said. "I really did think that the speckle paper was the best."

"I did consider the Speckletone Cream," Mother said.

I leaned my head over the table and rubbed my temple

with my fingers. Why had I not warned him not to mention the cardstock?

"Although the specifications listed it as two hundred and sixteen GSM card, it felt a lot flimsier than the two hundred GSM Ecru."

He looked at me with slight panic in his eyes.

"Did I see an Ecru?"

I withheld my sigh.

"No, Mother had the Ecru delivered earlier this week. I hadn't seen it until last night."

"Ah, I see," I swear he was hiding a grin. "So, what does the Ecru look like then?"

Like all the other damn cards, I bit back my automatic response.

"It's...quite similar to the ones I showed you earlier in the week."

He gave me a small smile, his little wonky tooth winking, showing that he appreciated my diplomacy.

"Very well. I guess Ecru is it then."

"See, Lucy. I told you he would agree."

Oh lord, Mother, he hasn't even seen it. He's just agreeing with you to avoid being told that he's wrong.

"Now, did you tell him about the other conversation we had last night?"

My stomach squeezed into a knot around the broccoli and green beans.

"No," I said. "Maybe you can explain your...concerns?"

I felt a simultaneous chill to my bones and a hot rush.

I caught sight of his tight jaw and winced.

"Well," Mother said. "I heard the fabulous news about Leila and Nate. Just thrilling, of course. But with the baby due in December and the wedding in February, well. I wondered how that will affect them on the wedding day?"

"That?" Joe asked. "You mean the baby?"

He raised an eyebrow at her.

I shuffled horseradish mashed potato around my plate.

"Oh, do stop that, Lucy. You are much too old to play

with your food." Mother said.

But apparently not too old to be scolded in front of my fiancé.

She returned to the previous conversation. "Yes, of course, the baby. What will they do with it? Will it be around for the ceremony? What if it spits up on Leila's dress? Worse, what if it spits up on Lucy's?"

"Well, it shouldn't show up. My dress will be pure white, remember?"

She shot me a burning look.

"I'm sure we'll be able to manage something in that regard," Joe said. "What do you think, Clinton?"

Dad raised his eyes from his plate and scanned each of our faces. I wondered for a moment if he had been following the conversation at all.

"Well, it is your wedding. If you want to have Leila and Nate, you should have Leila and Nate."

"Oh, Clinton, you really have no idea." Mother said. "It would simply be so selfish to make them have to think about Lucy and Joseph when they have a newborn baby to dote over. I was so glad that we had our wedding before I had Lucy. As my mother said, it would have been so difficult after she was born. All the late nights and early mornings. And my body simply never returned to what it was."

There it was, another reminder of my almost illegitimacy.

Joe looked momentarily stunned. "Well, that is all as may be, but we really do want to have Leila and Nate in our wedding party. We'll have to talk to them about it, and we may think about rescheduling the wedding to accommodate them one way or the other."

Oh lord, I really hoped Joe was calling her bluff.

It was Mother's turn to look stunned, and it swiftly turned to bluster.

"Oh, but you can't do that," she said. "Tell them they can't do that, Clinton!"

The whine in her voice was very unbecoming of a lady.

"Well, now, let's not be too hasty," Dad said.

"Don't worry, we won't be hasty," Joe said. "This is a big day for us. One we want to be able to tell our grandchildren about. We want to make sure we are making all the right decisions and have the right people around us on the day."

Mother looked like he had slapped her by throwing her own sentiments back at her. I sensed that things would go further downhill at great speed if I didn't intervene.

"So, has everyone finished their dinner?"

I stood and swooped my plate, which still contained half of my mashed potato, and Joe's off the table.

"Please change the subject." I whisper-begged as I bent over.

He stiffened, then nodded slightly.

"So, Clinton. How is your golf handicap these days?"

Dad, bless him, took the cue and swiftly took off, leading the conversation on tees, clubs and ball selection.

Mother stewed for a moment and then collected the plates from her side of the table, including Dad's, which still contained almost half of his meal, from underneath the cutlery he still held aloft.

"I'll help." Mother said as she led the way into the kitchen.

I prepared myself for a thorough ear bashing.

"How bad was it?" Joe asked in the car on our way home.

"Shrill. I don't know how anyone can speak so softly yet in such a high pitch. I feel sorry for the neighbourhood dogs."

He smiled ruefully.

"Sorry."

"It's not your fault. Next time we need to change the subject to Mother's dahlias or something, so she is kept at the table. I managed to put the rest of Dad's dinner in the fridge before she binned the scraps. Hopefully, he'll find it and be able to finish it now. Poor Dad."

I sighed.

"I really don't know what we're going to do."

The indicator started clicking as we approached my street.

"Registry office?" He suggested.

I was fairly certain he was only half joking.

"No, we can't do that. The church is already half fixed, and the deposits have been paid for the caterer and the photographer."

"We can still do the big day for your mum, but we can have our day, our way first."

It was very tempting.

"What would the point of it be, though?"

"So we can have it our way and then just let her choose everything for Valentine's Day."

We turned into my driveway.

I chewed my lip as I got out of the car.

"Like we're just acting for her? No, I don't think we can. I'll just have to make the most of the big day and get as much of my way as I possibly can. Damn, it's hard, though."

I unlocked my front door and let us in.

"I think I know what will help," he said.

"Oh?" I turned to him, definitely interested in his suggestion.

"A shoulder massage."

Bless the man. He was definitely right. We moved to the lounge room, where he sat on the couch, and I sat on the floor between his legs. I flipped my shoulder-length hair out of the way to give him easy access for the massage.

With the tension in my muscles easing, I could think more about the problem.

"Do you think, though...with the pregnancy...that dealing with my mum will just make Leila more stressed? Never mind the having the baby at the wedding thing, neither of us care about that, but having Mother yammering at Leila about all sorts of things wedding-related, surely that won't be good."

I chewed my lip after getting that out.

116

"You mean, the wedding prep, rather than the wedding, might be too stressful for them?"

"For Leila. Don't they say being stressed is bad for the baby? I know that being around Mum stresses Leila out. Mum can be really horrible sometimes."

Joe snorted. "Sometimes!"

I waggled my head in partial agreement.

"Why don't we sleep on it?" Joe suggested. "We still have some time—the decision doesn't have to be made right now."

February 14, 1:20 p.m.
Brace yourself

Bridget called directions to Wendy as she navigated her way through what I imagined was a full horde of zombies, but it could have just been a couple on a street corner. Who knew?

I discovered that my ability to keep track of where we were was almost non-existent when I was braced against the back seat of a car with only a narrow view of the sky through the rear passenger window.

"So," Bridget said, "What happened to those two in the deli with you? Were they fine this morning?"

"I'd rather not talk about it right now." Wendy said, "Just trying to get through this to make sure my family are okay."

"Okay," Bridget fell silent for a moment, then, "why do you think we're okay?"

"Bridge!" I warned, trying to mentally communicate with her that she shouldn't piss off the woman who was driving us away from the zombies.

"Right. Sorry. This is me up here on the left."

The car jerked to a stop.

"Do you always give directions with such short warning times, or am I just lucky?" Wendy asked.

Bridget gave a nervous-sounding giggle.

"People do sometimes tell me that I'm not great at giving directions."

I had rolled over onto my stomach from the sudden stop and found my face in the footwell, staring down a few fries that seemed a lot more than a day old and a parliament of Happy Meal toys.

Yet another reason not to have kids, I thought.

"Okay, let's roll."

I heard the two front car doors click open, and then the passenger door slammed shut. Bridget was definitely not a delicate girl.

There were two simultaneous clicks as the car's rear doors were opened, revealing the back of my neck on one side and what I feared was the entirety of my undergarments on the other. My fears were confirmed when the door was swiftly closed again, and a gust of air blew in to brush against most of my thighs.

Who said my wedding day would be dignified?

"Well," said Bridget. "I'm pretty sure I read in a book once that if you get stabbed with a barbed arrow, you should poke it the rest of the way through rather than yank it out."

"What?" I managed to angle my upper body into a twisted baby cobra pose in the back of the Micra.

"Because if you pull it, the barbed bits can snag on, you know, internal parts and cause more damage?"

I scrunched my eyes shut, trying to work out what she meant.

"I think she means your skirts are like the barbs on an arrow. You need to come out this way because your skirt has opened up, and you'll never get out again the way you got in."

"Right," I said.

My back complained about the angle, and I returned to facing down the Happy Meal dog toy.

"I think if you can get on your belly, you'll be able to commando crawl," Wendy instructed.

"You realise this is a $6000 dress, right?"

"You realise you're covered in blood and stuff, and you're spreading it into the back seat of my car, right?" She replied.

It was a valid point. The prospect of losing a few beads to her back seat upholstery didn't seem like much of an issue with context.

I shuffled onto my elbows, feeling my skirts twist around

me as I rolled within them. Oh, for a simple A-line skirt now. Wait, being realistic, what would be better would be a nice, bedazzled pantsuit.

"Can you brace your feet against the door and push a little?" Bridget asked.

"Um."

I poked my legs around a bit but found that my feet were now completely trapped in my train.

"Nope."

"Come on, commando time," Wendy said. "We've got incoming, and I want to get home to my kids and lock us all in." She fell silent for a moment. "There are words I never thought I'd say aloud."

I got up on my elbows and, bracing against a dip in the cushion, pushed off. And went nowhere.

I grabbed the edge of the seat and pulled, and still went nowhere.

"I'm going to open the other door and let the zombies pull you out in a second."

And that was enough motivation to get me to pull the upper half of my body out of the car and somehow defy the laws of physiology to get my bent legs through behind me. I somehow managed to end up sitting almost demurely on the lawn, although my bodice had slipped to dangerous levels.

I gripped the edges of the heavily beaded neckline and tried to pull it up, but with the rest of the dress beneath me, it was not going to work.

"Help me up," I said.

I raised my arms for them to pull but stopped suddenly when the danger in my bustier intensified to the point of wardrobe malfunction.

"Whoa," said Wendy. "Stop right there. We'll haul you from your armpits if we have to. I don't know about her, but I don't know you well enough to see what's going on under there."

"Oh, don't worry," Bridget said. "I don't know her well

enough for that either."

Wendy shook her head and grabbed me by an armpit, and Bridget hauled me from the other. I winced as they grabbed the raw flesh where the beading of my bodice had rubbed against my upper arm. I don't think brides are meant to be quite so active in their wedding gowns. Fighting zombies is clearly not part of the design brief.

I found myself upright, although my feet were still entangled in my train.

First, I yanked my bodice up to once again provide some dignity. Then I rustled my feet around within my skirts to find the bare ground beneath me. Finally, I spun a half circle to untwist my petticoats.

Feeling neat again, I nodded.

"Right, now what?"

Wendy handed me my umbrella and closed the back door of her car.

"Well, I don't know about you two, but I'm outta here! Thanks for saving me." Wendy said.

"Yeah, you too," I said.

Wendy was already at her door.

"Good luck with the whole wedding zombie thing."

She'd slammed the car door and was revving the engine before I had a chance to reply. Bridget waved as the tiny pink car sped off down the street and drifted around the corner.

May 2, last year
Bridesmaid betrayed

"Isn't it lovely out!" I said, tipping my head back and enjoying the sunshine.

Joe agreed with me and made his way across the deck to set a bowl of chips down on the little table.

"So good to get a few warm days before winter kicks in properly," Leila said.

She was stretched out on the outdoor lounge, knees kicked up over the arm and her head in Nate's lap.

The sun was shining on her face, and she looked stunning.

"So, what is the latest from Momzilla?" Leila asked, turning her face to me.

"Well, we finally discovered the difference between puce and goldenrod," Joe said.

My stomach clenched. It was time to come clean.

"We've decided the invitations and the napkins and the chair bows. I can't believe there can be much left to do now." I said.

"Do you have plans for dress shopping yet?" Leila asked. "That is always the biggest thing. I felt so much better about our wedding after I chose my dress."

"There are so many styles! How do you even choose?"

"I can help with that," Leila said. "Online look books?"

My stomach clenched tighter, and a lump rose in my throat. I looked at Joe. We had to tell them now.

"About that," I said.

Leila narrowed her eyes at me. Dammit, the woman knew me too well.

"What?"

"Well," Joe started. "We've seen how you guys have been over the last few weeks. We are so happy for you, don't get me wrong..."

He got lost then, so I took over.

"Lei, you've been so worn out in the last few weeks, and we know that stress is bad for you when you're pregnant and weddings can be stressful and dealing with my mother for you is like running a marathon up Mount Everest, and we don't want you to be stressed about how to get back in shape after the baby and all that rubbish—"

"Geez, Luce," Leila interrupted. She laughed, but it was brittle. "Get to the point already."

"I—we—really do want you both in our wedding, but we think it won't be good for you to be around my mum so much, so we're going to let you off the hook for the wedding. So you can focus on the baby."

She sat up abruptly. "Wait, what? You don't want me as your matron of honour anymore?"

"No, that's not it at all."

I vaguely noticed that the guys took a step back from us as I moved around, perched on the table and grabbed both of her hands.

"I do want you to be in the wedding, desperately, but the little nugget in there—" I pressed a hand to her belly, "—is so much more important and dealing with Mother, well. She isn't good for your blood pressure."

"You've got that right." She snorted.

She looked into my eyes, switching her gaze across my face.

"Are you sure this is what you want?" She asked. "It was your idea?"

I swear, my wince was only slight, but she caught it.

She flung my hands down and sat back.

"I knew it," she said. "She made the choice for you, didn't she?"

I looked around for Joe, hoping he could rescue me, but he and Nate had disappeared.

123

"I'm not going to lie. It was her idea initially." I said.

Leila snorted.

"But her reasons were totally different, it was all about fitting in the dresses and what to do with the baby, and I don't care about any of that. I'd buy a mini gown to dress the baby in. You could walk down the aisle with her in the pram for all I care. But I don't want you to have to deal with Mother for the next ten months!"

Leila leaned forward and took my hands again, "I understand where you're coming from. I don't agree with it. I could handle her."

I cocked my head at her.

"Alright, it would probably be difficult and would raise my blood pressure, which is less than ideal when pregnant, I know."

I leaned forward and hugged her and felt a jabbing through my heart.

She sighed and leaned her head on my shoulder.

"I accept your decision."

"I'm sorry," I said.

I was glad she was okay, but damn, it felt like I was betraying her. She was my best friend. And I was booting her from my wedding.

It was for her, though. Nobody else should have to deal with Mother.

February 14, 1:25 p.m.
Of cars and keys

The car groaned and turned over again. And didn't start again.

"Bridge?" I asked.

"I don't know," she said. "It does this all the time, but it always starts eventually."

I scanned the dusty dashboard, worn gear stick and webbed wing mirrors.

"When was the last time you had it serviced?"

She looked at me blankly.

"Serviced? Where you take it to a mechanic, and they check the engine and change the fuel filter?"

"Oh!" She said. "I thought only new cars needed that."

Oh lord.

"When was the last time you drove it?"

She scrunched her left cheek up as she thought. "Tuesday, maybe?"

I studied the grimy instrument panel and wondered if she could even read the speedometer.

"Wait...no, it was a Wednesday, about three weeks ago."

The remaining hope I had that we'd get anywhere in that car drained like the remaining volts in the battery every time she turned the key.

"Bridget, it's no good."

She sighed. "I'm sorry."

"It's not your fault."

My brain buzzed as I tried to think. There had to be something we could do, somewhere we could go. My house was about a 30-minute walk away, which was not appealing given the conditions, my clothing and my footwear. Plus, my house was locked, and my keys were in the overnight bag in the back of the limo, so even if we did get there, we'd have to break in.

My neighbours could be home, blind old Mr Kroger wouldn't be any good to me, but the middle-aged couple on the other side might be able to help.

Wait up.

"Neighbours!" I said.

Bridget looked at me a little blankly.

"Everybody needs good ones?"

"Yeah, do you know yours? Would they help?"

"Um, yeah, I guess. We could try the Iacopettas. They don't get out much, but Mr I has an old car he gets about in."

My heart sank when she described the car as old. My disappointment must have shown because Bridget hastened to reassure me.

"Oh, don't worry. It's old, but that car is, like, immaculate! I think they bought it when they had their first kid or something, or maybe when he retired...

"Anyway, he cleans it, like, every weekend and is always tinkering about with his engine. He's offered to look at my car a few times, too. Maybe I should have let him..."

She looked back at the car's dark instrument panel.

"Shall we go check then?" I asked.

She looked up at me like something else had been going through her head, and I'd jostled her out of it.

"Sure."

She didn't look or sound certain, but I didn't have time to worry about her. Time was ticking ever closer to the ceremony. I needed to get to the church.

Bridget made idle conversation as we crossed her browning front lawn to her neighbours. It was a big lawn. Actually, looking at it, she had quite a big house. I wondered how she could afford the rent.

"Oh, I don't pay rent. I own it. I lived here with my dad."

I suddenly realised that I knew next to nothing about Bridget, except she was my youngest bridesmaid and wore size 7 shoes.

I stopped walking in confusion. How had I never asked her about herself in the 9 months since Mother had asked her to be my bridesmaid. We'd spent hours together, but all we did was plan the wedding. I shrugged to myself and started walking. I told myself it didn't matter. She was only there to fill the space at the altar and help me get ready. I didn't need to know about her.

Something about the words I was telling myself didn't feel right. The texture was wrong. I got a weird pang in my side, and I didn't think it was from the corsetry.

Before I had time to psychoanalyse myself, we were at the neighbours' house and Bridget was knocking on the screen door.

The solid timber door was open, so Bridget called out after a moment.

"Mrs I? Mr I? It's me, Bridget. Are you home?"

We waited another moment, then Bridget opened the door. She turned and held it open for me, but I paused.

"Should we just go in?" I asked.

"Don't worry, I've known them forever."

I stepped into the house onto mottled coffee and white carpet. The walls featured a retro 60s wallpaper, and an old record player sideboard sat to the left of the door, opposite the entrance to the lounge room.

"The keys will be in the kitchen. Mrs I is probably in there too."

Bridget led the way through the lounge room to the kitchen, her silk skirts swishing on the low furniture.

"Perfect," Bridget said, scooping the keys up from the counter.

"Hang on, I know we're in a hurry, but shouldn't we still ask first?" I asked.

"Nah, Pepe lets me borrow his car all the time. He knows my car is a bit dodgy. As long as I don't take it when they have lawn bowls or on Sunday mornings, they don't mind."

I nodded. We turned back to the lounge room and saw

the couple's vintage TV. I guessed it was from the 1970s and was in a freestanding full timber cabinet with knobs and a speaker on the right-hand side. The set was on but muted. The screen was blurry, but it showed lurid movie special effects zombies and a news ticker along the bottom of the screen announcing that the zombie apocalypse had come.

"Did I miss something?" I asked. "I swear none of the zombies we saw today were green."

"Yeah, me too," Bridget said.

Bridget skirted around the coffee table to the tv and turned the volume knob just as the newsreader came on screen. When the newsreader also had a green tinge to her skin, I realised that it was a quirk of the TV, not the footage.

"We are receiving reports of people being affected by this condition on a global scale," she read. "There are pockets of people who are still unaffected, and we are receiving calls from these people."

"How do you even call a news channel?" I asked, picking up on the least relevant point of her report.

Bridget ignored me.

"As yet, we don't know the cause of the condition, although there are indications that it is transmitted through fluids such as saliva and blood."

Bridget and I locked eyes, then cast our gazes over our blood-spattered gowns. Well, if that was the case, we were probably pretty well on our way to being undead by now.

"There does seem to be a protective factor as we have heard of instances where the condition has not affected all members of a household." The newsreader continued. "The current advice from government health agencies is to stay where you are, monitor the conditions of those around you and barricade yourself somewhere safe.

"Lock all doors that can be locked and barricade any windows that are low to the ground. Our service will continue broadcasting advice as we receive new information."

I stared at Bridget, wondering what the best option

would be. I wished I hadn't left my clutch bag with my phone in that damn supermarket. I would have really liked to be able to call the church, or even Joe, just to see what was happening out there.

My attention was drawn to a picture above the mantelpiece, and I focused on the photo.

"Wait, I know them. Mr and Mrs I, don't they volunteer at the library?"

Bridget shrugged. "Maybe."

"Yeah, they do. I see them every week. They are so sweet together."

They had been coming together for years and spent a couple of hours sorting and reshelving books. They had to be in their eighties. It was so lovely to see them working together.

Before I could explain this to Bridget, the newsreader drew my attention again.

"We have just received another communication from the government. They are advising everyone to stay indoors, avoid contact with people outside of their immediate household and avoid movement of any kind."

A besuited woman appeared on the screen, and the ticker identified her as the Chief Public Health Officer.

"This is a rapidly evolving situation that appears to be life-threatening. We don't know if we will be able to ensure the recovery of the affected persons, so our advice at this time is to avoid contact with people and take extreme care to avoid exposure to any body fluids..."

My concentration was broken by a sound behind me, and I suddenly realised that we were going against all government recommendations.

May 16, last year
Private Pools and public meetings

"What are the new developments this week?" Leila asked.

I looked at each person in the coffee shop and sipped my flat white while I considered my answer. I'd removed her from the wedding so she didn't have to deal with Mother drama. It didn't seem right to complain to her about all the decisions.

"Well," I said. "We chose the cardstock for the invitations last week and finally chose napkins and tablecloths this week. DO NOT mix up the word napkin and serviette in front of Mother is all I want to say about that.

"She is now getting samples of cutlery and plates from the caterers for the dinner service and will prepare for menu sampling soon."

"What about your honeymoon?"

I brightened. I had completely forgotten that we'd get a honeymoon.

"You know, I hadn't even thought about that! Mother has been focusing me so much on the ceremony that I forgot about the honeymoon."

"Alright! We can plan the honeymoon!"

Leila offered me a high five.

"Do you have your laptop?" She asked.

"I do," I said.

I reached into my bag and pulled out the laptop, and she moved to sit next to me instead of opposite me.

"I highly recommend the place we stayed in Fiji. We had to get a heap of travel vaccinations before we went, but it was spectacular."

She gave me the hotel's name, and I searched for it.

"I think it might still be the wet season there in February. The weather was pretty horrible when we were there. But face it, you won't really want to go much further than your villa anyway."

She gave me a cheeky wink before turning back to our search.

"Here, this one!" She pointed to a link for the hotel they had stayed at. "The more expensive rooms have their own pools right off the balcony of your private villa."

My eyes watered at the price.

"Yikes!"

Leila's smile curled higher. "But don't you have savings? And your mother said she was paying for the wedding? So you can blow your portion on an exxy honeymoon."

Her smile was downright devilish now.

"Plus, the flights are dirt cheap, so you're practically saving money compared to going to Europe or the US."

I shook my head at her. She was a crafty woman.

"Alright, let's put together an itinerary, and I'll show it to Joe."

We spent a happy hour planning day trips and choosing the best value luxury accommodation in Fiji. I felt like we were back on even ground again.

Until my phone rang.

'Love hurts'.

"Hi Mum," I said.

I forced some cheer into my voice against the heavy stone of dread that had formed in my stomach.

"Lucy, darling, where are you?"

"I'm out for coffee with Leila. Is there somewhere else I should be?"

She sighed.

"Lucy, I told you I was arranging a brunch for your bridesmaids today."

I opened up the calendar on my laptop. There was no

entry in the diary.

"There is nothing in my calendar Mum. When did you organise this?"

"Almost a month ago, Lucy. Really, you need to pay much more attention."

"A month ago?"

I racked my brain. Nope, I had nothing.

"Honestly, the girls have been dying to meet you all this time, and you haven't even arrived yet."

I bit back a sharp response.

"I didn't know, Mother. Give me the details, and I'll come straight there."

She told me the location. Thankfully it was within walking distance, although it was in the opposite direction to my car.

I hung up.

"What has she thrown you in now?" Leila asked.

I answered without thinking.

"Some bridesmaid meeting she apparently organised a month ago and thinks she told me about, but she definitely didn't."

"A bridesmaid meeting?" Leila asked. "That she organised a month ago?"

I shrugged. "Apparently. Man, if I am still talking to her on the wedding day, I—"

I suddenly understood Leila's point. A bridesmaid meeting that Mother had organised when Leila was still going to be my matron of honour. And Mother hadn't invited her.

Shoot.

"Oh Leila, I'm—"

She held up a hand to stop my apology.

"Don't worry about it, Lucy. I know she never wanted me to be part of the wedding anyway. She must be happy that she got her way."

"No, no. It wasn't her choice, remember?"

"Whatever you have to tell yourself, Lucy."

She folded up my laptop and held it out to me.

"You'd better go. You don't want to be any later to *meet* your bridesmaids than you already are." She paused. "Do you even know who they are?"

"Umm...err."

"I thought so. Have fun, Lucy."

She pushed my laptop into my hands and turned away.

I was about to speak when 'Love hurts' came from my phone again.

Dammit!

"Lei, I'll call you later, okay?"

My best friend just gave me a half wave as I grabbed my satchel, rejected my mother's phone call and turned to leave the café.

I fumed as I stalked to the restaurant where the brunch was being held. Mother had stepped way too far over the line this time.

We hadn't even discussed the bridal party in detail yet, and she'd organised this meeting without telling me or inviting Leila.

I entered the restaurant with a full head of steam, ready to create a scene that would leave Mother sleepless for weeks.

I spotted Mother's blonde head at the back of the restaurant. She was facing away from me at a table with five other women. I didn't immediately recognise the four younger women from across the room, but I knew that the fifth was Joe's mum.

I wavered in my resolve to stand my ground.

"Leila." Joe's mum, Amanda, smiled at me. "Isn't this exciting! I'm so glad your mum invited me to meet the bridal party. Dorothea, it was so thoughtful."

Amanda was a truly lovely woman. She did not deserve to see me have a temper tantrum at my mother.

Nor did the other women at the table, three of whom I did not know.

"Lucy, sit. Now that you're here, we can start."

I counted to 10 in my head as I was sitting down to hold my temper.

"Great," I said. "Hi, Kendall."

Yes, my horse-faced cousin was apparently going to be one of my bridesmaids. Brilliant.

"Ladies, our bride." Mother announced.

"Lucy, Nora will be your maid of honour."

Mother pointed to a woman who looked about my age, with shoulder-length, mouse-brown hair.

"She's been a bridesmaid three times already."

"Nice to meet you," I said.

"You know Kendall," she said to me. She turned to the other bridesmaids. "Kendall and Lucy are cousins."

Kendall reached out to bump knuckles with me.

"This is Perry."

Perry had a bleached blonde pixie cut and heavy eye make-up.

"And Bridget. She's the youngest of the bridal party, this will be her first time as a bridesmaid, but I'm sure the others will guide her in her duties."

Geez, she was making it sound like being a bridesmaid had as much responsibility as performing transplant surgery.

"Great, nice to meet you all."

I managed to be polite, if not warm, during the brunch, which fortunately included sparkling wine with our bruschetta.

The women seemed nice enough, but I was not impressed about Mother springing them on me. Or choosing them without talking to me about it.

I was developing a headache from the sparkling wine when the bridesmaids prepared to leave after we finished our meal.

Mother stood and prepared to leave too.

"Mother, may I have a word with you before you go?"

Mother looked at her watch.

"Oh, Lucy, I must rush, bridge, you know. I would have

had time if you hadn't been late."

"Mother, you didn't tell me."

"Oh, don't start that again."

I thanked the restaurant staff as I followed mother between the tables and out to the street.

I caught her up.

"Mother."

I grabbed her wrist to stop her.

She turned an appalled face on me.

"Lucy, you have terribly poor manners today."

"Mother, your manners aren't that great today either. You sprang a brunch on me with people I don't know who you have apparently appointed as my bridal party without discussing it with me. I'm a little upset."

Her face fell, finally. Maybe she understood my point.

"I can't believe I'm hearing this!" She said. "I've put in so much work for you, and that's what you have to say about it? I didn't see you trying to make these decisions."

"I *did* make those decisions. I wanted Leila, and you tried to convince me to drop her and even organised for her replacement before I did so." I appealed to the greatest power that moved Mother. "That was terrible manners and quite a social faux pas."

She took a step back.

"Well." She put her hand to her throat. "I guess you are right. I did show terribly poor manners."

It wasn't an apology, but the admission was the closest thing I could expect.

"However, you can be grateful that these decisions have been made for you, and Amanda will speak to Joseph today about securing his groomsmen too.

"It's all coming together."

She was right. It was. And I was sick of fighting with her about all the decisions that needed to be made.

February 14, 1:33 p.m.
Falling

We turned from the news report to locate the noise behind us.

The 'tink' was from the little ceramic mermaid being knocked over as the doily beneath was dragged aside by the dangling limb of the old lady zombie.

No, no, no, not Mrs I.

Ah, damn, Mrs I was definitely a zombie. She normally used a brass-headed cane to walk around and was always well-presented. I could have sworn her hair was perfectly coiffed the second she sat up in bed in the morning.

The reason her hair was always neat quickly became clear; her hair was full of curlers, some half dangling from her head.

In her undead state, her limping walk was turned into a half bob, the old lady bobbing up on her left foot so she could swing her right leg forward without bending her right knee.

The strange mode of movement was almost silent.

And that was not a point I should not have been reflecting on while she crossed the room towards us with outstretched arms and drool coming from her mouth.

Bridget and I finally took our gaze off the zombie formerly known as Mrs I and locked eyes ourselves.

The front door of the house opened straight into the lounge room and was now directly behind Mrs I. Our easy exit was blocked.

"The laundry," I said.

Bridget nodded and took off back through the kitchen to the laundry. I'd barely had enough time to gather my skirts before she reappeared, propelling herself backward through the laundry door.

"Mr I," she said in explanation.

I didn't ask any other questions. "That way, look for a bedroom with a big window."

I pointed her to the other door out of the kitchen, which opened onto a corridor, letting her go first in her more manoeuvrable attire.

The passage held small side tables with figurines and photographs. My dress left a passage of ceramic carnage behind me as I sent Mrs I's knick-knacks flying in my wake, but I didn't think that would do much to slow down the elderly zombies.

Crunching sounds followed me towards the bedrooms, proving my theory.

Bridget ran out of a bedroom as I turned into the passage. She moved into another and shouted.

"This one looks good."

I entered the bedroom seconds later, my moment of hope falling as I saw the window she had found.

A little over a metre off the ground and 2 metres wide, the sliding window would normally pose no problems. Any other day, I would have no trouble. But with a hoop skirt?

"I can't get through there. I'd need to change my clothes."

"There's no time to change. I don't even have time to unlace you from that dress so you can strip. Hurry up and get over here!" Bridget screeched.

She was trying to lever a piece of dowel out of the window track. Her acrylic manicure was not helping her efforts.

"Wait one sec," I said.

I slammed the bedroom door shut and searched the room for a prop. The door had a round handle, so the ornate chair wouldn't be any help to stop it from turning. There was a freestanding wardrobe, but I wouldn't be able to move that if it was empty and I'd had three Weet-Bix for breakfast.

The bedside tables were too far away. My only remaining option was a waist-high ceramic statue of Venus emerging from the clamshell. Sans clamshell.

Why would anyone want that in their bedroom?

I dragged Venus to the door, she was heavy, and the door opened inward; she should buy us some time. How much time was anyone's guess.

Bridget had opened the window and was trying to punch out the flyscreen when I reached her. I picked up the dowel from the ground where she had discarded it.

"Step back," I said.

Fear in her eyes, Bridget did as I instructed.

I swung the dowel at the window screen like it was a pinata stick, and I was a six-year-old after candy. While it wasn't broad enough to give enough force to knock the screen out completely, I managed to tear a gash down the middle.

"Go," I told Bridget.

She didn't wait to be told twice.

She climbed onto the bed, stepped to the bedside table and then up onto the windowsill. Once there, she pressed her shoulder against the screen to widen the hole enough to let her through.

She balanced for a minute, looking down at the ground below. She teetered, then leapt, landing with a thump. I was relieved when her head never disappeared from sight, even when she braced her knees for the landing. The fall/leap/drop wouldn't be too far.

I climbed onto the bed, wobbling wildly on the uneven surface with the small contact points of my heels.

"Can you yank out the frame of the screen?" I asked.

Bridget reached for the screen, but her nails and approach angle made it impossible.

I eyed the hole in the screen. Well, if I dove out headfirst, it might slow my fall.

As if I had predicted the future, I was forced to do exactly that when the sound of a shattering Venus rose above the grunts and groans of zombies, and the door let out a slow squeak.

In a moment of panic, I lunged, not thinking about where or how I would land.

As predicted, the flyscreen slowed my fall. To the point of stopping me altogether when my hoop skirt lodged itself across the window, too wide to fit between the opened panel and the frame.

I screamed. In anger, in fear, in sadness. My scream covered all emotions. It was an equal opportunity scream.

It kicked up a notch in the fear section when I felt something touch my leg.

"Calm down," Bridget shouted to be heard over my scream. "It's me. I'm trying to get you out of the window."

Her voice was somewhat muffled by the silk.

Sure enough, I realised the hands up my skirt were warm, not the ice cold of the undead.

She had managed to yank free some of the dress itself so she could access the springy metal hoops of the skirt beneath.

"Get ready to fall. I'm going to fold the hoops."

I had only a few seconds to decide how best to fall before she released me, and I slithered from the window like a newborn foal.

I managed to roll into the fall and do a somersault, so I wasn't injured. I did end up tangled, with the biggest hoop of my skirt springing up over my head.

I sat dazed for a moment, then reached up to grab the hoop. A hand grabbed mine instead and dragged me to my feet.

"Come on!"

Bridget dragged me around the side of the house and down the pressed gravel driveway to the garage.

May 27, last year
Guests

"You want to invite *how* many people?"

I'd almost choked on air when she told me the first time; repeating the number was necessary.

"About one hundred and forty." Mother said again.

"How? Joe and I only have seventy on our list combined?"

"Well, we must invite the Kostecki family because we were invited to Ramona's wedding. And the Michaels are practically royalty at the Country Club. We can't have a function without inviting them."

"But, Mum, it isn't about the Country Club. It isn't even at the Country Club. It's my wedding to Joe."

"But the engagement party was at the Country Club."

"Because you booked it there without even asking me about it! Mum, we don't want to have a huge wedding. We were only going to invite thirty before you started planning it."

"Lucy." Her tone was cold. "I would thank you not to speak to me that way. Your father and I have generously offered to pay for this wedding. I expect you to allow us to add to the guest list."

"But Mum, the cost of the wedding is just about doubling with all the people you want to invite. It's too much!"

She put down the pen and notebook she was holding to look at me, drilling into me with an intent stare.

"Lucy, I have always regretted that we had a small wedding. I don't want you to have the same regrets.

"We will be inviting all the cousins, aunts and uncles and influential people in town, and you will still be able to add your small group of guests."

I raised my eyebrows. I could still add my small group. How gracious.

"Okay, then, let's combine our lists."

We tallied numbers for a total of 275 guests.

"Hmm," Mother said. "Are you sure you want to invite Vanessa from the soup kitchen?"

"Mum! Yes. This is *my* wedding. I'm letting you invite a heap of people I don't even know. Joe and I have people that we would like to invite. If that pushes us over the limit, you need to adjust your invite list, not ours."

She sniffed.

"I'll speak to your father about the numbers."

I was sure she would.

"Now, about the tablecloths." She said.

"Huh? I thought we decided on those a couple of weeks ago?"

"Well, we did, but I'm just second-guessing."

I settled in for another hour of discussing the pros and cons of Ecru over cream and decided to just choose the relevant arguments, like the guest list, and let her have her way in everything else.

It was the only way I could see to make the next 7 months tolerable.

February 14, 1:45 p.m.
On the road

Bridget slid the huge steel panel door of the garage open. Despite the size, it glided smoothly and easily. It was either well-oiled, or Bridget was stronger than I thought she was. I took a moment to study her shoulders and back. She actually looked well-muscled. I was a little surprised.

I was more surprised by the little rocket of a car hiding in the depths of the garage.

The car was white and boxy in the 70s and 80s style, with a small rear wing. What I could see of the car was immaculate. Shining white paint and a small logo on the boot lid that said 'Spirit'. The Toyota logo in the middle was glistening chrome and the car looked as though it had been polished every day of its life.

"Wow," I said.

Bridget turned and smiled.

"Isn't it great?"

I nodded and walked to the passenger side.

The car was low to the ground, and I could clearly see Bridget over the roof.

She put the key into the door lock, and the tab on my side popped up.

I opened the door to assess the beaded seat covers, immaculate brown carpet and gleaming interior surfaces. Although the car was much older than Bridget's, it was in much better condition.

The footwells were free of the takeaway containers that had littered Bridget's and showed no sign of ancient French fries. I sat, relieved that there was nothing in there to further soil my dress.

Bridget put the key in the ignition and turned. The car

purred to life. Bridget's gear change as she ground the car into reverse was not quite as smooth.

We bunny-hopped backwards down the driveway to the street. When we passed the front of the house, I glanced towards the window we'd escaped through. Two bodies jostled at the window, arms pushing at the screen that was barely hanging in the frame now. Fortunately, the frame was quite high, almost to the petite Mrs I's waist. She wouldn't be getting out through the window. Mr I, however, was quite tall, so his centre of gravity was higher than the windowsill. As Bridget turned the car onto the street, the last piece of the screen was torn from the frame and Mr I toppled forward out of the window, landing on his head and shoulder.

I winced. That was not a gentle landing for an old man.

However, before Bridget had put the car in first gear, his arms were moving, and he was pushing himself upright again.

Bridget put the car in gear smoothly this time but didn't release the clutch.

"Come on, Bridget. Let's go!"

I looked at her and found lines of tears and streaks of mascara running down her cheeks.

"Hey," I said, gentle this time. "Are you okay?"

She sniffed noisily and ran the back of her hand across her nose and cheek.

I reached into my bodice and pulled out a tissue that was not folded quite as neatly as it had been when I placed it there.

She accepted the tissue and dabbed at her eyes and nose. A little speck of zombie blood smeared across her cheek as she did.

"Sorry," she said. "I just...need a second. That was hard to see."

Mr I had gained his feet now and was slowly lurching towards us.

"I understand," I said.

I didn't, but I knew that saying so was the only way to get her to move the car.

"Why don't you tell me about them while we are driving?"

She sniffed again, then nodded. She placed both hands on the steering wheel, gently released the clutch and applied the accelerator. We moved past the house, Mr I, in the yard, and Mrs I, in the window, tracking our progress with their lifeless stares.

Bridget let out a last, great sob before she changed gears and pressed the accelerator harder.

"Like I said before," Bridget said, "I've known them forever. My whole life. They were there when my Mum left and then when my dad died. They've been so supportive. They wanted me to go off to university and be a physio, but I was too scared to leave town. I worried that if I left, I would lose them too, and now I have."

She managed to hold herself together somehow. I wanted to feel some sympathy for her, but given everything else happening, I didn't have any emotions left to spare.

"Okay, I think I'm alright now," she said. "Let's get you to the church."

She gave me a watery smile.

We drove in silence for a few minutes, moving through the streets at a speed that was probably slightly higher than the limit.

The roads were mostly empty, but there were a few cars parked on the street. I spied one car that had stopped with two wheels on the verge, but deep tyre ruts indicated this was normal.

We made good progress towards the middle of town and were nearly on the home straight to the church, when Bridget was forced to stop. We were back on the main street, close to the supermarket, and the road had become completely impassable.

Cars were parked on both sides of the road, but three cars had also stopped diagonally across both lanes. Bridget might have been able to navigate between the cars in the small Toyota, but the real problem was the zombies.

They were penned in the spaces between the cars, appearing to have herded themselves in. There must have been a hundred bodies milling about, plus a few on the ground.

I studied the undead to see if I recognised anyone but found I couldn't focus on any one person for too long. The gore, vacant stares and damage to faces and bodies were too much.

Bridget put the car in reverse and performed a quick three-point turn.

"Where are you going?"

"To find a path that isn't blocked. I imagine a couple of major roads are both like this. We'll have to skirt around town to get to the church."

I nodded. "Okay. Let's go."

June 10, last year
Winking smiles

"Now, I have compiled a list of photographers and videographers available for the wedding day." Mother said. "Fortunately, they weren't all booked out because the wedding is on Sunday, but you must make a decision quickly, dear. We're running out of time."

Only because you chose the wedding date and made it less than 12 months away, I thought.

"Do we really need a videographer?" I asked. "A couple of my friends had a DVD made of their wedding, and they don't even have a DVD player to watch it on anymore. That's the sort of thing that will get outdated really quickly."

Mother tsk'd.

"Of course, you need a video, Lucy. Think about your grandchildren."

Right now, I didn't even want children. And if I did have them, I didn't think I wanted to live through all the pre-wedding trauma by watching the video with them.

"But the money, Mum," I said instead. "The reception will cost over a hundred dollars each for two hundred and fifty people, plus we haven't found my dress yet. And then there will be shoes and accessories and—"

"Never mind about all that, Lucy." Mother said. "It's no secret that I didn't get any of those things at my wedding, and I've always been a little sad about it. I won't get to share my special day with you or your children.

"I know I haven't mentioned it before, but there is no need to worry about the money. I've been saving up for your wedding for years. Seventy-five dollars a week since you turned sixteen. And your father has some extra savings that we can use too if we need."

I tried to calculate the savings, but my brain was too fried, so I pulled out my phone. She'd been saving $75 a week for almost twelve years. That was $3,900 per year. A total of almost $46,800.

"You think we'll spend more than $45,000!"

Mother sighed and reached her hands across the table towards me.

"Lucy, darling, I know you don't understand this, but I really just want to give you a spectacular wedding and help you get started in your life together."

"Mum, we could spend half that and have a wedding that we're happy with, and you could gift us the rest. That's half a house deposit you want to spend on the wedding!

"It's too much."

"Nonsense." Mother said. "I won't hear any more about the cost. It's our gift to you.

"Now, let's look at these photographers."

She showed me photo galleries on the websites of eight wedding photographers. Then overrode my decision and said we should appoint the third one she'd shown me.

By that point, I didn't even care.

"Now, one last thing about the photos." Mother said.

I braced myself. I had a feeling this wouldn't be good.

"Well, you know my friend Josie, Josie Vida? She's an orthodontist."

I did not know where this was heading.

"Yeah?"

"Speak properly, Lucy. She was looking at the photos from your engagement party the other day and mentioned that it would be so simple to straighten out that crooked little tooth of Joseph's.

"She could fit him with a retainer and said that he would barely notice it and the tooth could be straightened out in about four months, so there is plenty of time to do it before the wedding. What do you think?"

She had finally rendered me completely speechless.

"Mum, I'm willing to let you have a say about a lot of things for the wedding, but cosmetic dentistry is way too far."

"But Lucy, those finer details bring it all together." She used her wheedling tone.

"I hardly consider adjusting the alignment of Joe's teeth to be a 'finer detail.' "

"Really, Lucy, you are too sensitive."

I couldn't stay in the room with her any longer.

"Mum. No." I said as I stood. "You will not mention Joe's teeth to me again, and you will not mention this to him."

I walked to the door and turned back.

"I have let you make a lot of decisions for my wedding but taking aim at our appearances is going too far. Don't expect us at dinner tomorrow.

"I'll talk to you next week."

I walked from the room and the house and climbed into my car. I sat for a minute. My hands shook too much to drive.

Honestly, the woman was so image-conscious and self-centred. Joe's wonky tooth was one of the things I found most appealing about him.

He was so kind and generous and caring that his wonky tooth was one of the things that reminded me that he wasn't too good for me.

She had found one point of the wedding planning I would not waver on.

February 14, 1:55 p.m.
Around town

Bridget safely navigated to the road that ran parallel to the last row of houses in town and made her way south.

The car skimmed along the rough country road like a power boat, regularly bouncing us from our seats and slamming us back down again.

"Where do I need to turn?" Bridget asked after a few minutes.

"I don't know! This was your idea!"

"Well, it was either this or being stuck on the wrong end of the main street."

Logically, I knew this, but logic didn't have much space in my brain at that particular moment.

"Yeah, yeah. But I had almost no idea that these roads existed, and I have no way of navigating for us."

Bridget shrugged. "We'll work it out."

We continued bouncing along the road for a few more minutes. I felt that silence grow awkward as we flew along between the paddocks.

The odd cow looked up as we passed, and I was momentarily thankful that they didn't seem affected by whatever was going on with the people. Zombie cows seemed like they would be entirely too difficult to deal with.

"I'm sorry about your neighbours," I said after we passed yet another paddock.

"Thanks. They're good people," Bridget said. "They took care of me like I was their granddaughter."

"You said your dad died?" I asked.

"A couple of years ago," Bridget said. "It was really sudden. He had a heart attack. I was at school, and he was home alone. When I got home, he was already gone."

God! That poor young woman. She must have been in her last year of school, only 17 or 18.

"I'm so sorry. That must have been hard."

She gave a small smile. "It was. Thankfully Dad had paid the house off already, and there was plenty of money to support me while I finished high school. But Mrs I was the one who actually kept me fed with real food and motivated for school."

"What did your dad do?"

"He was a hedge fund manager."

That explained why Mother had singled Bridget out as a bridesmaid. Her dad must have been minting money.

We fell into silence again.

A few minutes later, we approached a t-junction.

"What do you reckon?" Bridget asked. "Keep going or turn here?"

I mentally mapped the town layout and the time we'd spent driving. By my estimation, we should be close to or level with the southernmost streets of the town.

"Turn right," I said. "If we haven't passed the southern outskirts of town, we should have at least passed the traffic jams."

Bridget turned right.

We crested a rise, and I saw houses on the right-hand side of the road, but I wasn't familiar with the surroundings. However, I suddenly recognised a sign a few minutes later.

"Wait, that's the sign for the church. Turn here." I said.

Bridget tried to make the turn, but I'd told her way too late. I was used to approaching the church from the other direction and hadn't seen the landmarks.

We screeched to a halt about 15 metres past the turnoff.

"Wow, now I understand why Wendy was complaining about late notice earlier."

Bridget performed a U-turn on the narrow road and made her way back to the turnoff.

"It's only about twenty minutes from here," I said.

According to the analogue clock on the dashboard, it was only 2:15 p.m. I should make it to the church well before the ceremony, which was scheduled to start at 3:00 p.m.

I might even be able to clean the blood off my face, and the worst of the gore off my dress before walking down the aisle. Excellent.

I looked over at my driver as we fish-tailed around a corner.

"Bridget? Are you okay?"

She looked pale, and beads of sweat had formed on her forehead.

"Hmm? Yeah," Bridget said, "I'm alright. Just a bit of a headache. I think it's just that I haven't eaten enough today."

She raised a shaking hand to swipe some hair from her forehead. She almost missed the next bend, sweeping to the outside curve on the wrong side of the road.

"Bridget?" I asked again. "Are you sure you're okay?"

We were already a kilometre down the road to the church.

I was so close.

Then Bridget grunted, the car swerved, and we careened off the road, heading straight towards a thicket of gum trees.

June 20, last year
A little loss

I had just put the last mug in the cupboard and pushed the dishwasher drawers and door shut when I heard the door open.

"Hey, babe," I called. "You're back quickly."

Joe had left my place only about 20 minutes earlier to play basketball with Nate. Not a formal game, just shooting hoops.

He walked into the kitchen, his face pale, and leaned against the doorframe.

"Whoa! What's wrong?"

He rubbed his face with his hand and then held his arms out to me.

As I neared him, I saw tears in the corner of his eyes.

"Oh, Luce, it's..." He paused and suppressed a sob.

"Nate called. They had...they had an ultrasound this morning...the baby..."

I looked into his face and was filled with fear, a cold shard of ice stabbed through my chest.

"Oh, Luce, honey, they couldn't find a heartbeat."

I scanned his eyes, although it was hard as my own were filling with tears too.

"No," I said, wishing and hoping I could undo what had happened with that one word.

He nodded softly, and I looked away, putting my head against his chest as I cried. I cried for her, and I cried for her and me as I realised that I had irreparably hurt our relationship for no reason.

None of the reasons I had for removing her from the wedding party were valid anymore. None of the reasons

Mother had were valid anymore, not that they had been in the first place.

And above all that, my friend was hurting, and I didn't think I would be welcome to be there for her as she grieved.

I thought of all those things and the little life that wouldn't be, and I cried.

February 14, 2:15 p.m.
Walking with open eyes

I barely even had time to swear after we left the road. I whacked the gearstick into neutral, pulled the handbrake on and grabbed the steering wheel, trying to pull the car back onto the road.

Bridget had gone limp in her seat, but her hands still hung over the steering wheel and tangled with mine as I pulled the wheel towards me.

My efforts weren't quite enough to save us from hitting the trees, but the driver's side took the brunt of the force rather than it being a head-on collision.

I fell against Bridget's shoulder, hitting the crown of my head on her chin. A swear word tumbled from my lips, and tears sprang to my eyes.

I blinked a few times to clear the fuzz from my head and then sat to assess the situation.

Bridget's head rested against the window, which was remarkably intact. We'd hit a tree in the middle of the rear driver's side door. The car had bent around the tree, and the window of the rear door had smashed. Remarkably, the front half of the car was free of damage. Despite that, I didn't think the car could be driven further. The rear half was clearly bent out of shape.

"Dammit," I said.

My head was swimming from the impact, my shoulder hurt from the seatbelt, and it looked like I was another bridesmaid down.

Just as I thought this, Bridget stirred.

Her fingers twitched in her lap, and she let out a groan.

"Bridget? Are you okay?"

I had flashbacks of asking my other bridesmaids a

similar question earlier in the day, and I shuddered.

Bridget groaned again, and her eyes fluttered open.

The whites of her eyes were bright red. Her hands tensed into claws. She reached towards me.

I screeched, and my hand caught my skirt as I tried to undo my seatbelt. My panic rose, and my chest grew tight as I fumbled.

Finally, I found the release, pulled my seatbelt away and threw myself at the car door and my freedom. A wash of air over my shoulders as a dove indicated that Bridget had been moments away from successfully attacking me.

Or, at least, the zombie who had once been Bridget.

I reached back to grab my umbrella from the passenger footwell, narrowly avoiding another lunge from Bridget.

My stomach clenched again. A pang of something I couldn't identify washed over me. Maybe a little anxiety about getting married?

I shook off the feeling and rose before also shaking off my dress. The hem had collected some leaves and sticks when I dove from the car.

I turned back to close the car door and saw Bridget lunging across the gear stick, held back by her seatbelt. I slammed the door and jumped back.

That was one zombie that wouldn't be joining the masses.

I looked to the road and pondered my next move. The area was a mix of paddocks and small collections of trees. The church was about 4 kilometres south. I could walk that far.

I waded through the tall grass on the verge, collecting more grass seeds in the beaded panels of the dress. I was beyond caring.

I reached the packed dirt road and looked at my train dragging along the ground behind me. It would be a lovely shade of dust within a short time, but there was very little I could do about that. Bridget had partially bustled it in the alley and hadn't had a chance to do more. I was just glad that it hadn't come undone when I fell out the window.

I had walked maybe 500 metres when the weight of the dress became a burden. Who would have thought 3,000 Swarovski crystals would be a problem? If I'd known I'd be dragging it 4 kilometres to the ceremony, I'd have chosen a classic silk A-line.

I rounded a bend in the road and saw a car parked on the left, facing away from me.

Maybe it was wedding guests who had stopped on their way. They could give me a lift.

I didn't recognise the car, and I couldn't tell if there was anyone in it as I approached.

As I drew closer, I saw that the window was down on the driver's side, and a hand was hanging out over the windowsill. I could be in luck!

The hand flapped in and out of the window and tapped on the car body as I approached, tapping out a song I didn't recognise.

On one particular wave, I spied a small moustache tattoo on the person's index finger and realised who it was.

Vanessa, the manager of the soup kitchen. I hadn't seen her in so long. My heart rose. She was a legend. I was so glad that Joe and I had convinced Mother to add her to the guest list.

"Vanessa!" I collected handfuls of my skirts and hustled to her car.

Her hand stopped flapping for a moment, then began moving more furiously.

"I am so glad to see you. You wouldn't believe what a morning I've had! All my bridesmaids are zombies, and the last one crashed the car I was in. Can you take me to the church?"

Vanessa hadn't spoken by the time I reached the driver's door. The reason for this became clear when I saw her blood-red eyes.

Great, I would have to keep walking.

Vanessa's hand reached out of the window again, her

fingers stretched out in a silent appeal.

Her outstretched hand reminded me of all the times she had reached out for a soup ladle or dirty dishes or just to help me up off a milk crate at the end of a long shift.

Tears pricked at my eyes.

This woman had given so much. How was my first thought that she wouldn't be taking me to my wedding? What had happened to me? Where was my compassion?

I'd seen almost a hundred zombies today, including people I was close to, and here I was, still focused so completely on my wedding.

I collapsed in a puddle of tulle on the verge of the road, ignoring the dirt, grass seeds and thousands of dollars spent on my outfit, finally seeing the real problem and not liking it.

It was me.

I was the problem.

The zombie apocalypse wasn't just an inconvenience that had arisen on my wedding day. It was a terrible disaster for all of humanity.

And here was me, moaning about how it ruined my plans.

I didn't recognise myself. When had I become this heartless bitch?

I cradled my head in my hands and cried.

12 months ago, I had been a kind person. I volunteered my time at a soup kitchen, stitched quilts for homeless people and was nice to my friends. And this wedding had weeded all of those kindnesses out of me.

It was a wonder that Joe still wanted to marry me at all.

I looked at Vanessa, tapping on the door and reaching into space. This woman had been so kind and considerate that she had even parked her car perfectly on the side of the road before becoming a zombie. I mean, who did that?

I cried harder at the loss of this friend.

God, who else would I lose? Who else was already lost?

I felt myself slipping into grief.

Zombie Vanessa finally brought me out of my grief with a particularly loud thump on the car door.

I smiled as I thought of what she would say to me if she'd found me like this at the soup kitchen.

Probably something like, "Yeah, these really bad things have happened today, but you aren't going to get anywhere in that puddle of tulle, are you?"

And she would have been right too.

I had already come this far. I had outlived my bridesmaids for some unknown reason. I needed to find out who else was still alive.

Although I'd had a completely different motivation for saying it earlier, the point was valid. My family and most of my closest friends would be gathered at St Columba's Church in under an hour.

The best thing to do was pick myself up, get to the church and then work on being a better person tomorrow.

"Vanessa," I said, although I knew she couldn't understand me. "I'm so sorry about the last few months. I've handled this wedding all wrong. I just followed Mother instead of standing up for myself, and I lost myself in it all.

"I'm sorry I wasn't there for everyone. I know it must have been hard. I'll do better. I promise."

I looked at her then. Her vacant, red eyes stared. Her arms reached out, but her body was restrained by the seatbelt.

She would offer no absolution, but maybe she would offer inspiration.

Vanessa never faltered while there was work to be done. She might take a minute to rest once service was over and all the jobs were done, but I had never seen her stop while there was soup to make, people to be served, or dishes to collect or wash.

I stood, using my umbrella as a prop as I untangled my skirts. I didn't even bother trying to clean them this time, just turned from the car and kept walking.

February 14, 2:30 p.m.
Just another paddock

I walked another kilometre that felt like six.

My feet throbbed in my shoes, my armpits were raw from the beads and my back hurt from dragging the weight of the dress.

And it was hot. The afternoon sun was blazing down, and I could feel sweat running down my back. This lady doesn't glisten. She perspires. Heavily.

Like a mirage in the distance, I saw a vehicle appear in a nearby paddock. It was red and black, and the engine was idling as it sat unmoving. A quad bike.

I scanned the fence line for a gate, gap or space I could squeeze through. No luck on that front.

I spied a tree stump a couple of metres away. It was only about 30 centimetres from the fence and stood almost as high. There was also a pine fence post close to the stump. If I was lucky, I could climb onto the stump, step to the fence post and then step down into the paddock.

Surely, I was due some luck?

I waded through the grass on the verge again, making a beeline for the stump. It seemed that I was lucky as there was a branch from the tree on the ground next to it that I could use to step up onto the slightly wonky stump.

My perspective seemed to have been off as the tree stump was not as large as I had thought. I had thought I would be able to stand on it, but the stump was only just big enough for one of my feet.

I mapped my path. Fallen branch, tree stump, fence post. Okay, I could do it, but it would have to be in one continuous motion. I wouldn't be able to stop once I'd hauled myself up onto the stump.

I used the umbrella for balance as I stepped onto the branch. I made it up onto the branch with no problem and balanced on the balls of my feet. Leaning my weight more heavily onto the umbrella, I gripped my skirt high with my left hand and raised my right leg onto the stump. I teetered for a moment, balancing on my right leg as I tried to rise, bringing the weight of my body and dress up to the height of the stump.

When I was steady, I took a slight leap to get my left leg onto the fence post. I landed my left foot exactly in the centre of the fence post. I cheered myself on internally.

But I cheered a little too soon.

The momentum from the jump carried me forward as I brought my right foot to meet my left, forgetting that there was no foothold. I awkwardly pushed off with my left leg, hoping to land on both feet on the other side of the fence without falling.

My dress had other ideas.

The skirt caught on the barbed wire of the fence. It barely held before it tore, but the moment that it held was enough to throw off my trajectory, and I landed on my knees instead of my feet. I fell forward, catching myself on my forearms.

I was stuck in a weird reverse cobra pose, with my forearms pressed into the rough stubble, knees on the ground, and feet suspended in the air by the front of my dress, which was now snagged on the fence. I wriggled my legs forward, wincing as my dress was ground into the dirt. Well, it had tripped me this time; it probably deserved it.

The hem came loose with a tearing noise that brought that pang back to my belly. My poor dress.

I crawled a little way, the stubble poking through the skirt of my dress to my knees and shins. When I felt I was far enough from the fence, I scooched back to get my feet clear of my skirt, pushed myself to a crouch and then a standing position. I took a few steps and retrieved my umbrella from where I'd flung it as I'd fallen.

I tried vainly to brush the dirt from my knees but settled for picking the stubble from the beading instead.

I scanned the paddock and found the quad bike where I had first seen it. Sitting in the middle of the paddock with no rider in sight.

I approached the bike cautiously. It hadn't driven itself to the middle of the paddock. Someone had ridden it there.

"Hello? Is there someone here?"

My questions were answered by the dull thrum of the engine and bleating sheep in the next paddock.

I stepped closer to the quad bike. I still couldn't see anyone nearby.

I heard a noise when I was close enough to mount the bike. A horrible slurping and tearing from the other side of the bike.

I peered over the seat and spied a woman dressed in jeans and a flannel shirt. Her long hair was pulled back in a ponytail, which was pulled through the back of her cap. Her hands were bloodied and pressed into the fleece of a sheep stretched out on the ground. Her face was buried in an open wound on the animal's side.

An involuntary shriek left my mouth, and I froze. The woman paused in her attack on the sheep carcass and turned her head slowly towards me. Her body remained still, but her head and eyes slowly tracked my position.

Ice ran through me, and I prayed that she wouldn't notice me. But even if she didn't, I still had to attack her. She was close enough to the quad bike that it would draw her attention when I accelerated away, exposing me to attack.

She surveyed me for a moment but turned back to her sheep after a moment. I breathed out a heavy breath and thought about my next move. Her head was closest to the bike's rear tyres, and her feet were at the front tyres. I judged that trying to attack her from the rear would be my best option.

I moved around to the front of the bike with my umbrella

wielded and ready to attack.

Through some zombie sixth sense, she noticed me. She was on her feet before I reached the front of the bike. I didn't even see her move. One moment she was hidden by the bike; the next, she was up and lunging for me.

She wasn't smart enough to move around the front of the bike first, so her progress was halted as she bounced into and off the wheel arch. However, the impact pivoted her enough that she could move forward to the front of the bike and then turn to lunge at me. I sprang backward, somehow managing to not land on my skirt.

I prodded at her with my umbrella, but she lunged again a moment after I moved and the umbrella was knocked from my grip, flying off in an arc.

I dodged her again, but this time my right shoe caught in a deep rut in the soil and my ankle rolled awkwardly as I landed on my side. I hurried to remove my foot from my shoe, which was still stuck, so I could shuffle away from the next attack.

The zombie lunged and lost her footing. I managed to roll away, so she didn't land on me. When I stopped, my skirt was wrapped around my legs, my bodice was twisted and the discarded, bejewelled Louboutin was within reach of my right hand. I sat, grasped the heel by the arch in the centre of the foot and yanked it free of the dry soil.

The zombie lunged again, and I held the shoe up in front of me with both hands, spiked heel towards the zombie.

The zombie lunged. I aligned the shoe and...squelch. The shoe went through her left eye, deep into her eye socket and embedded in her skull.

Her body went limp, and I was forced to roll again as she collapsed to the ground. Fortunately, I rolled the other way this time and untwisted my dress.

She had fallen on her front, and I rolled her over so I could retrieve my soiled shoe.

The heel came free with a schlunk, and I wiped the zombie's brain and eye matter from the heel.

The heel appeared to have done some damage and rendered the woman properly dead rather than undead.

I pulled the shoe back onto my foot. Wincing as the back scraped against a couple of raw patches of skin. They were comfortable but not designed to be worn while stumbling along dirt roads and through rutted paddocks.

I eyed the shoes of the woman in front of me.

Sturdy work boots.

While I didn't want to think of myself as one of the boot thieves from history's fields of war, it wasn't like I would take her boots to sell them. I was taking her boots to give myself the best chance of survival.

I shuddered at the thought of wearing a dead woman's shoes. I mean, I bought clothing from op shops, and I had no idea whether the people were dead or alive. But there was a distinct difference between potentially buying clothing that had belonged to a dead person and literally taking the shoes off a corpse.

"You're doing all this for your family." I reminded myself. "For Joe, Lyon, Mum and Dad."

And Leila, I thought, but didn't say. After all, Leila and Nate weren't invited to the wedding.

I shook off that thought to contemplate later.

I squatted down to remove the dead woman's boots.

February 14, 3:05 p.m.
Borrowing

I baulked at wearing her socks.

I pulled the boots onto my bare feet, wincing when I felt their warmth. The poor woman obviously hadn't been undead for long.

I studied my Louboutin's and decided to hold onto them for future use. I retrieved my umbrella and approached the quad bike from the same side as before, so I didn't have to look at the sheep carcass again.

I lifted my skirts to mount the quad bike. The hoop popped up in front of me, covering the fuel tank and pressed back by the handlebars. Fortunately, the hoop dipped down on the side, so while my borrowed boots were visible, the dress covered most of my legs to the top of my knees.

I carefully pulled my train onto the tray on the back of the quad bike and tossed my Louboutin's in a small wooden crate strapped down in the same area.

Right, I wondered, now how do I drive this thing?

I gripped the handlebars and noticed a small lever under my right thumb. I pressed it, and the engine revved. I guess I found the accelerator. Okay, but what about the brake. There were two handlebar levers that looked like bicycle brake handles. They must be the brakes. Now for gears. I looked around on the handlebars for something that looked like a gear stick before finally finding the lever under my left foot.

Here goes, I thought.

I kicked the lever down, and the bike promptly lurched forward and stalled.

Right, there was probably a clutch somewhere. I pressed

the red started button on the handlebars. Nothing happened. I tried again and twice more. The damn thing wouldn't start again.

I thought back to Dad's lessons on driving a manual. Clutch, gear, accelerator, brake. What was I forgetting? I knew there was something. Like I'd agreed to something and then promptly forgotten what it was.

I thought about turning off an engine.

'Neutral, handbrake, park, off.'

That was the mantra I told myself every time I parked my car. "Neutral!"

I knocked the gear selector up a notch and pressed the starter again. The bike started and hummed away beneath me. This time, I released the clutch slowly and applied the accelerator slowly. I lurched forward and gave a fist pump.

Yes! I was finally on my way.

February 14, 3:10 p.m.
Understanding

I opened the throttle and took off across the paddock, my veil billowing out behind me.

I didn't know where I was going but I aimed for the fence line closest to the road. Surely there would be a gate connecting to the road or at least a neighbouring paddock.

I reached the southernmost corner of the paddock, sure enough, there was an open gate to the next paddock. The next paddock was also filled with wheat stubble, so I stuck to the flattened dirt adjacent to the fence as I rode. Finally, I reached the fence for the next paddock and was relieved to find a gate leading to the road.

I pulled up, opened the gate, drove through and closed the gate behind me. Just because the world was descending into chaos didn't mean I should let someone's sheep wander onto the road.

I motored onto the road but kept my pace moderately slow. There was every possibility that I would round a bend and find a car on my side of the road.

The 5-minute drive was a 20-minute quad bike ride, but I finally crested the last rise before the church and stopped. The tiny valley opened up before me: the church nestled in a tiny hollow, the overgrown rectory beside it, a cemetery in the foreground and a giant white marquee to the right of the cemetery. The marquee was incongruous in the quaint surroundings. It ruined the rustic setting of the church.

I had a momentary flare of anger at myself for not standing up to Mother. Every decision about this day had been hers, from the church to the reception and place settings.

I let her railroad me with emotional blackmail, somehow

166

allowing her to convince me that I should have the wedding of her dreams.

I realised that jealousy for her sister had also been a factor. The story she had told of me wanting to be married here since I was a flower girl for my aunt had been a manifestation of her own desires. My aunt's wedding had been lovely. Mum and Dad had been married at the registry office because I was on the way.

I sighed, thinking of the long-ago fantasy of Nate marrying us in a park. Too late for that now.

The more pressing issue was where everyone was. The car park was hidden behind the church and a row of trees, so I couldn't tell how many people had arrived. However, the two vintage cars that Joe and his groomsmen planned to drive to the ceremony were parked neatly at 45-degree angles in front of the church, ready for post-ceremony photos with the bridal party. Perfect.

I shook my head. Photos really were not a priority right now.

Movement near the side of the church caught my attention, and I saw someone walking hurriedly, dressed in yoga pants and a teal t-shirt.

I crinkled my brow. It was lucky I wasn't worried about photos. That outfit would certainly stick out like nothing else.

"Lucy!" I berated myself.

As I watched, another figure in jeans, a man, emerged from the side of the church, walking backwards. He took two steps into the open before a lurching figure followed him. A man in a suit, arms outstretched, blood smearing his white shirt.

The man in jeans shouted something, and the woman bobbed down and pulled on something. The zombie tripped and faceplanted on the pavers surrounding the church. They worked together to roll him off the path and into the bushes.

A moment later, they were gone. There was no sign of

167

the living or the undead.

I wondered if I was hallucinating from dehydration.

Or hunger.

I figured I had been running on adrenalin since Kendall, Perry and Nora had become zombies so many hours ago.

I wondered how many hours it actually was. I hadn't worn a watch and didn't have a phone. Based on the sun, I guessed it was almost 3:30 p.m. Well past time for me to be at the church.

I hit the accelerator and rode on down the hill. I spied another car on the side of the road. This time it was one that I recognised.

Leila and Nate's little blue Corolla was parked neatly on the side of the road, about 100 metres from the church.

What were they doing there? I was so awkward with them after their miscarriage that we hadn't invited them to the wedding. I didn't know how to treat the grieving couple.

Joe didn't feel as awkward as me, but he agreed that we could leave them off the list because we hadn't seen them in the months leading up to the wedding.

Plus, we already had more than 250 people invited to the wedding. Most of whom Mother had invited because they "were paying after all."

I groaned at myself. I'd let her turn me into a horrible person. I'd let her turn me into *her*.

I had made such a horrible mess of this. And I didn't know who I would get to make amends to. Certainly not Vanessa.

I parked the quad bike next to Leila and Nate's car and turned the engine off. I realised how quiet it was without the engine noise and had a horrible feeling that I had made a mistake.

Zombies reacted to noise, and I had just ridden up on one of the noisiest vehicles you could find in the area.

I dismounted and listened for a moment. Only the rustling of the leaves and chatter of birds came to my ears. It seemed I was safe, for now.

I turned to the box on the back of the quad bike to assess my weaponry.

I had the blue-handled umbrella, my Louboutin's, a length of twine, a pair of shears and an old bottle of Jif cleaner. Not much to get on with.

I didn't need my expensive shoes, but they had been useful. I cut a length of twine with the shears. I made a slipknot and slid this over the shoe, tightening it over the arch. I repeated with the other end of the twine and the left shoe.

I held the shoe bola in my left hand and the umbrella in my right and stepped away from the quad bike. I walked around the car to check for signs of life. It was empty, with no signs of blood in the interior, but there were a few thick smears across the bonnet.

I shuddered at the smears and accompanying dents. It didn't take much imagination to work out what those were from.

As I walked to the passenger side, I noticed that the car was parked adjacent to a trail through the scrub that went perpendicular to the road for a few metres before turning to the right. I studied the path and the road, assessing my options.

The path was probably a lesser-known option, but the road was wider, potentially offering more zombie dodging opportunities, and likely to be a more direct route to the church.

I took the road.

February 14, 3:35 p.m.
Choices

I rounded the first bend in the road and immediately realised I had made the wrong choice.

A staggering of zombies was...staggered down the next 20 metres of road. Between 10 and 20 zombies were spread across the road, forming a maze of bodies that I would have to dodge and not draw the attention of.

I clamped down my emotions as I surveyed the men in suits and women in formal dresses, bright block colours and floral prints. These people were dressed to attend a wedding. Our wedding.

I grabbed the back of my dress in my left hand and moved back as quietly as possible with a cathedral train. Hopefully, the path through the scrub was clear. I advanced quickly along the straight sections but slowed at the corners, listening for movement ahead and holding my umbrella at the ready.

The trees ahead of me were thinning out when I heard the noise.

A quiet shuffle of footsteps around the next corner. I stopped and waited. The shuffle came again. Two quick steps and then silence.

Wait to defend or move to attack? I wondered.

The decision was made for me when I heard the footsteps again, coming quickly. I moved to the side of the path, inside the curve, umbrella held in both hands, ready to defend myself.

I was glad I had stepped aside when a woman in a teal t-shirt rushed around the corner, a baseball bat in hand, ready to swing.

"Leila." Her name came out as a whisper, reverential.

She was an avenging angel in yoga pants and a t-shirt that matched my wedding colour scheme.

"Lucy!" She shrieked, then clapped her hands over her mouth.

I rushed her, grabbed her and squeezed her tight with both arms.

"I am so glad to see you," I said. "This has been such a horrible day."

Leila grabbed the back of my head and pulled me in closer.

"Oh, I bet, you poor thing. You've been planning this wedding for so long and today has been horrible."

I pulled away from her, shame washing through me. That wasn't what I had meant, but it shamed me that she would think it was.

"No, Leila, it's not that. God, I don't even know where to start. I am so sorry. I was such an asshole to you! I just felt so awkward about booting you from the wedding. Then you lost the baby, and I didn't know what to say or how to get you back. And Mother had organised these other bridesmaids, who were horrible, by the way, and I didn't know what to do.

"Leila, I want you to know that I am so sorry about the baby. That was so shit. You should be a mum. You should have a little baby to snuggle and love and feed and..."

I stopped when I heard her sob.

"Oh shit, and now I've made you cry. I am such a horrible person."

She shook her head.

"No, no. It's okay. It's just that no-one has said anything like that to me. It's been all, 'oh it happened for a reason' or 'it just wasn't the right time' and I've just felt like screaming and asking why. And nobody ever has an answer to that question."

I pulled her in again and we cried on each other's shoulders for the baby she had lost. We released the months of tears we had wanted to share together, but I hadn't known how to approach her. We held each other and cried for a moment before a grunt drew our attention.

We looked down the path towards the road, still hugging, but there was nothing to see.

We released each other, but I clasped her hand tight in mine. We took a few steps to the corner she had rounded and peeked around.

One single zombie stumbled up the path. Grunting and groaning to himself as he took a wobbling step.

As one, Leila and I retreated around the corner.

"Shall we save the rest of the deep and meaningful for later?" She asked.

I nodded. "Yes, but let me just say I'm sorry again. For everything."

My heart squeezed again. I had been such a horrible friend.

"And, Leila, I would like to ask you something as I asked once and should have asked again. Will you be my bridesmaid?"

"You don't seem to have many other options." She said.

My gut clenched.

"But I love you and you're my best friend. Of course I will be your bridesmaid."

I let out the breath I had been holding and moved to hug her again, but she held out a hand.

"We have something else to attend to before we start hugging again."

She pointed down the path to the corner.

I nodded. "Right. Uncle Rowan."

She cocked her head at me.

"Yeah, I recognised him. An uncle on my mother's side. He was never a nice guy. I think I'll enjoy belting him with my umbrella."

"He's a big fellow. I think we might need to take him down together."

We poked our heads around the corner and assessed the situation.

"I reckon..." Leila said and sketched out a quick plan.

"Sounds good."

I turned so she could unclip my veil from my hair.

"Good grief, where have you been with this? It has bugs in it."

"Oh, I rode a quad bike here," I said.

"That was you?" She said, her jaw slack.

"Uh-huh." I smiled.

Her face turned thunderous. "Lucy! Why weren't you wearing a helmet?"

I gaped at her. I hadn't even thought about a helmet. There wasn't one there. Man, that was reckless.

"I'm sorry!" I said, "I won't do it again."

"You got that right!" Leila said.

She glared at me a moment longer before returning to her task.

"Alright, he's nearly at that wider section. Are you ready?"

I nodded and she handed me one end of the veil.

"Ready? 3...2...1...go."

We sprang around the corner, trying not to tangle or get tangled in my skirts.

We bundled our ends of the veil together and charged down the path towards Uncle Rowan. He reached a portion of the path wide enough for us to pass on either side of him. We bobbed down to lower the outstretched veil to the height of his shins, caught him in it and kept running.

There was a moment of resistance as the veil pulled taught and then it was ripped from our hands as Uncle Rowan went down, taking the veil with him.

"Yes." We said together.

We shared a high five and surveyed the damage. Uncle Rowan was down, and he looked out too. Unconscious possibly, or properly dead. We had no way of knowing and no desire to check if we did.

Leila had tied my shoe bola around a belt loop on her jeans. She released it and passed it to me. We had left her baseball bat and my umbrella on the path behind us, so she scurried back past the floored zombie to retrieve it. I had been right before when I thought we were nearly where the trees of the scrubland thinned out. The path opened up not too far ahead.

Leila re-joined me and we moved forward cautiously.

So far today, with a few exceptions, I'd never found one zombie alone.

We reached the tree line and I realised that this path led to the cemetery. Bit of a morbid walking trail, but whatever.

And what was creepier than a cemetery? A cemetery scattered with the undead bodies of my friends and family who were dressed to attend my wedding.

High-end fashions and expensive suits were now full of snagged threads and covered in dirt, grime and blood. I hoped none of the suits were hired because nobody would be getting their deposits back. Not that I guess they cared in their current state.

"Which way?" I asked Leila.

She was standing at my shoulder and scanning the rows of the cemetery too. Trying to map out a path that we could follow.

Her eyes and mouth moved silently as she mapped out a path.

"I think we enter that row, near the black headstone with the photo. Turn right at the giant angel statue, go two rows forward and turn left at that old concrete headstone. Then it's a straight run to the church from there."

I mapped out the path as she spoke.

"Looks good," I said.

I grasped her hand again before we moved off.

"Leila…" I wasn't sure what I wanted to say. "…Thank you."

She gave my hand a squeeze. She let go and led the way through the cemetery.

February 14, 3:43 p.m.
Explanations and entry

The first two segments of the planned route through the cemetery were perfect.

We went in at the black headstone with the picture of the lady and then right at the giant angel statue. It all went awry when we reached the old concrete headstone.

As if zombies had the power of premonition, three appeared within lunging reach of our planned turn.

"Quick, turn here," Leila said, turning a row earlier than we had planned.

There were three zombies about ten graves ahead front of us, we dodged between two headstones to dogleg over to the next row and I offered silent apologies to the spirits whose eternal rest we were disturbing.

Two zombies to our left, four to our right.

Another dodge, more apologies and more squeezing of my skirts between headstones.

We turned right, heading to the church again. The path was clear.

The group of zombies appeared from behind a giant memorial. First one, then three more, followed by another two.

We skidded to a stop just metres away from them. I looked back and found that three were closing in behind us.

We couldn't squeeze through any gaps on our left and the row of graves on our right was swiftly filling with zombies too.

We were surrounded.

"Whose idea was it to invite so many people to this wedding?"

"I believe that was your mother."

I winced. I deserved that barb.

I turned to Leila.

"Leila, I..."

She held up a hand. "No time. I'll run along the side of the path. You run straight at them. Bust through however you can and head to the church."

The church was less than 50 metres away, and I wanted to weep at how close we were.

Just five or six more zombies and we'd be through. The horror would be over, and I'd be reunited with Joe.

"Alright, let's go."

I charged the group of zombies that was slowly approaching us, reaching up to pull my great-grandmother's hat pin from my hair.

"Something old."

I stabbed the hat pin through the cheek of the nearest zombie.

The woman staggered and fell away from the front of the pack.

"Something new."

I swung the makeshift bola of my $2,000 shoes around my head before striking a zombie in the face with them.

"Something borrowed."

I lifted my skirts and kicked the next zombie in the chest with my borrowed boots, knocking him into the bodies behind them, taking them down in a pile of writhing limbs.

"Something blue."

I gripped the blue handle of the umbrella in a javelin grip and threw it at the nearest zombie.

My aim was terrible, but the pointed tip of the umbrella caught him in the crotch. Apparently, that is not as effective an attack in the undead male as in living men. He continued to lurch forward with the umbrella protruding from his upper thigh. Damn, that thing had bedded deep in his thing. I didn't like my chances of getting it back.

Out of weapons, I turned, gathered the remnants of my cathedral train and ran, weaving my way through the headstones.

"I'm clear!" I shouted. "Get to the church. We can barricade ourselves in."

Pounding feet sounded behind me, a streak of teal overtook me and Leila reached the chapel door 20 seconds ahead of me.

Twenty sweet seconds for her to fling one door wide to give me entrance and hurriedly slam it behind me to lock us safely in the small vestibule.

"You are dressed much more sensibly than I am." I puffed.

My bridesmaid turned and smiled at me.

"We made it." She said.

"We did." I smiled. "We're only a little late."

I had lost track of the time much earlier in the day and had no idea what the time actually was.

"It's right for the bride to be fashionably late."

I laughed outright, then stopped and gripped my ribs. "Dammit, don't make me laugh. This dress is so tight!"

"Sorry," she said.

"Now, look at me. Let me see you."

I straightened my spine, threw back my shoulders and looked her in the eye.

"Um," she said. "In the circumstances, you look gorgeous."

I glanced down at my tattered, dirt-encrusted and blood-stained dress.

"That's probably all I can hope for."

"Right, let's go get you married to the love of your life."

"Before we do, do we have time for that talk?" I asked.

She looked at me.

"I don't even know how many apologies I owe you. I was horrible when I booted you from the wedding."

She held a hand up. "The logic you used was sound, though. Dealing with your mother for all those months would have been a nightmare, even without worrying about the baby."

I grimaced. "She has been pretty horrible. And I just agreed with her the whole time. I was such an idiot."

"Well, I wouldn't say idiot, but I did try to warn you."

I sat on a small bench in the vestibule. "Yeah, I know. I never realised how controlling she is. Everything has to be her way, and if you don't agree, she emotionally blackmails you. She insisted we make decisions about things and then told us we were wrong so she could prove that she was better.

"I was so blind."

Leila sat next to me and put her arm around my shoulder.

"It can be hard to see faults in people you love."

"I think it will be hard to see anything to love through all her faults now."

"It will be okay."

I nodded.

"I don't know what level okay will be, we'll have to actually find out what is happening in the rest of the world at some point, but we'll survive," Leila said.

I looked at my friend in awe of her positivity.

"How can you do it? How can you have been through so much grief and still be positive about life?"

She pulled her arm from my shoulder and shrugged. "What else can you do? I don't get to hold him close, but I'm still Richie's Mum. I owe it to him to keep living in his name."

"Richie," I said the name like a prayer. "I didn't know that was his name. He was a boy?"

She nodded. "Yeah. He was...he was so perfect."

She looked down at her fingers in her lap. I watched as she poked her right thumbnail under all of the fingers on her left hand. She repeated the process with her left thumbnail and right hand. She took a deep breath in, and her shoulders shook.

"He was so perfect...his heart just stopped beating. Our grief counsellor encouraged us to give him a name to help us cope with his loss."

"I'm so sorry I wasn't there to help you."

She reached out and squeezed my hand but didn't, or couldn't, look at me.

"I understand. Nobody wants to talk about pregnancy loss. It's one of the last taboos in society."

My heart squeezed.

"Why did you come here today? To our wedding, even though we'd been terrible friends."

Leila took her hand back and repeated the fingernail thing, still avoiding eye contact.

"We…" She took a deep, steadying breath, her shoulders shaking with the effort, "…we didn't come here for the wedding.

"I had actually forgotten that it was today. Nate and I have been in our own little bubble for the last couple of months."

I nodded, not that she could see.

"So why?"

"We came to visit Richie." She shrugged. "We'd been out to visit when this church was chosen for the wedding. We loved the bushland surroundings and the wild roses over the pastor's old house. There was peace here. When we had to choose somewhere to bury Richie, this place seemed right."

Tears sprung to my eyes.

"We come here every few weeks. It's part of our process. We tell Richie how much we love him and miss him and give our grief space to just be."

Her breath hitched and her fingers fell still.

"My aunt had a miscarriage when she was about my age, but they didn't give women the opportunity to grieve then. Just told them it was nature's way and there was nothing they could do. The pent-up grief nearly destroyed her.

"Nate didn't want that to happen to me. And he needed to deal with his own grief too."

"So you were just here to grieve for your baby, and you

got caught up in the drama of my wedding? Leila, I'm so sorry."

Would I ever stop apologising to my friend?

She finally looked at me. Tears were unashamedly running down her cheeks.

"Don't be. It isn't your fault. None of it is. None of it ever was. It wasn't your fault that you didn't know how to help me. We were never taught." Her voice wavered as she continued. "It's like if we knew how common pregnancy loss is, women would never want to get pregnant. It would be too terrifying."

It made a twisted sense, and my tears flowed freely too.

"Anyway, we came to visit Richie. We saw the marquee and realised it was your wedding day. And then we saw the zombies here and decided to stay in case you needed any help."

I hugged her again.

"Thank you."

We hugged for a few minutes before Leila gave a loud sniff.

"Right, so. I've helped you battle off a horde of zombies with a baseball bat. Shall I walk you down the aisle now?"

I released her from the hug but grasped her hands and squeezed them for a moment. We smiled at each other through blurry, tear-filled eyes.

"Alright, let's do it."

We both wiped our eyes with the back of our hands. I probably made an even bigger mess of my face.

She stood and walked to the double doors that led into the chapel. I took my place behind her.

There probably wouldn't be any harp music playing as I walked down the aisle to Joseph, but it wouldn't matter. Not in the circumstances. And I never wanted any of that anyway. That was all Mother.

Leila reached forward and grasped the handles of the doors separating the vestibule from the chapel. I saw her shoulders rise and fall as she took a deep breath before pulling the doors wide.

She gasped.

I craned my neck around her and peered in. The chapel was filled with friends and family who turned in our direction when the doors banged open.

Their faces were slack.

Their eyes bore the vacant stare of zombies.

February 14, 3:59 p.m.
Two doors close

Leila grabbed the left-hand door, and I scurried over to the right-hand door so we could shut them both against the stares of the undead.

Leila grabbed a tall candlestick and threaded it through the giant ornate door handles.

"That should hold them off for a while," Leila said.

"Wait, did you see if Joe was in there?" I asked. "And where is Nate?"

"Nate should be holed up in the vicar's house next door. He was going to see if he could find Joe. I was heading to the car to see if I could head off the limo when I ran into you."

"But did you see the altar?" I asked.

She shook her head.

"We have to look again," I said.

We left the candlestick in the door handles and carefully pulled the doors towards us, creating a gap we could peer through.

Few of the zombies had moved in the minutes since Leila had flung the doors open and we'd hurriedly closed and barred them.

I tried to count heads. There weren't a lot of people in there, maybe 50? In a church big enough to easily fit 250 seated.

I couldn't see any of my direct family members. Most of the people in the room looked like members of the Country Club. All of my parent's vintage, dressed in clothing that cost more than my car and likely to have arrived at least an hour early, so they could solidly criticise everything before the ceremony started.

Nobody was standing at the altar, and the front few pews were empty, indicating that my parents, brother and groom were not in their correct places.

I pushed my door shut and Leila followed my cue.

"So, the old rectory?" I asked.

Leila nodded her agreement.

"Let's go find our men."

We moved to the external door. But I halted Leila before she opened.

"Wait, two things. One, check if the coast is clear. Two, we need weapons."

She nodded.

The vestibule had no windows and the only door opened on the side of the church furthest from the rectory. Our view out the door wouldn't give us much information on all of our path but it would at least show how much danger there was in our first steps.

We searched the tiny room for defensive weapons.

Leila picked up her baseball bat from the floor.

I picked up a hefty candlestick that was the pair to the one we had barred the doors to the chapel with. It was made of cast iron and about 120 centimetres tall. I pulled off the candles and wielded the stick with the spiked candle holders pointed forward.

There was a thump behind us. The door to the chapel rattled.

"Time to go." Leila said.

"Yep."

We walked to the external door and Leila slowly opened it. Peering out the crack as it opened.

"All clear," she said.

She stepped out of the door, and I grabbed it with one hand so I could manoeuvre my skirts through. Unfortunately, the door slammed when I let it go.

The bang made me jump.

I glanced about for any zombies that had been alerted to our presence.

No sign of movement on this side. Leila moved down the path until she could peer towards the rectory.

"Okay, we're clear for now. Come on."

I followed her as quickly as I could while wearing what felt like 18 kg of dress and wielding 10 kg of steel.

Although more comfortable than the Louboutin's, the boots had started to rub. The adrenalin rush from the run through the cemetery masked the pain from the blisters, but that was wearing off. I was left feeling light-headed with pain in my feet.

The rectory was set back from the road a little further than the church and had a long garden overrun with wild roses. We'd planned to take photos in the garden. Mother and I had made sure the path to the old front door and a patch of ground against the front wall.

We crossed the open ground towards the garden and turned into the front yard.

Where we were confronted by a dozen members of the catering team. Men and women in the black-and-white butler's uniform crowded around the door to the rectory and beat against the walls in an attempt to get in.

"Oh crap," I said.

Leila had already stopped and taken a step back towards the entrance of the garden. I was not prepared and stumbled back. I flung my arm out, forgetting the candlestick, and caught the stone wall a glancing blow with the solid steel leg of the candlestick.

I cringed at the ringing clang of the impact.

The zombies at the cottage stopped hammering and turned to us.

We froze.

The leading zombie held his face tilted upward and sniffed the air as if he was sensing the vibrations of our breathing and scenting us.

A string of swear words circled in my mind.

A terrible pause fell across us. A horrible tableau of vicious attackers and hunted prey in the moments before the attack.

And then they moved.

February 14, 4:15 p.m.
Refuge

The closest waiter surged down the path towards us.

I dodged onto a secondary path to the right. Leila dodged to the left. My path only extended a few metres along the wall before disappearing into the wilderness of rose bushes.

At least I wouldn't be surprised by any zombies from the rear.

The path was tight, but there was just enough room to swing my candlestick. I turned back to watch the main path and waited for the first zombie to come within swinging reach.

Leila had disappeared into the garden on the other side of the path, and I prayed that she was safe.

The waiter reached the entrance to my path. I waited for him to shuffle one step closer and then swung, hitting him in the neck with a crunch of flesh and bone. The man crumpled to the ground.

I stepped closer to the path where two more zombies were coming my way. To wait or attack? I chose to attack.

I wielded my giant candlestick like a double-ended battle staff. I poked the first zombie into the overgrown garden beds on the right with the candle end and whacked the second zombie in the same direction with the feet end.

A scream sounded from my left.

Leila!

I hurried back down the path to trace her steps. I reached the gate and followed the left-hand path around the garden. My heavy boots pounded on the stone pavers and my skirt snagged on outreaching brambles as I rushed to her aid.

I found her cornered against a wall of the cottage. Three zombies closing in on her. Two on the ground at her feet.

Blood seeped through her t-shirt on her right shoulder, and she held the baseball bat in her left hand. As far as I could remember, she was right-handed.

This was not good.

"Oi, you lot," I shouted, hoping that Leila would be smart enough to stay silent as I drew the zombies' attention.

I momentarily regretted my decision when two of the three zombies moved in my direction. I saw Leila swing her baseball bat with enough force to knock the third zombie down before giving my attention to the two zombies stumbling towards me. I gripped the candlestick with both hands and swung forehand at one zombie, a woman, and backhand at the man on my left.

I stepped over the bodies in front of me and reached for Leila. She held her shoulder with her left hand.

"What happened?" I asked.

"One of them bit me."

I tamped down my horror and fear. There would be time for worrying about that later.

"We'll clean it. You'll be okay."

She nodded but winced in pain.

"Come on, let's get to the door. The zombies must have followed the boys there."

I led the way this time. Leila was close behind me.

We followed the wall of the building around to the front.

I shrieked when a hand appeared from nowhere and grasped my arm.

"Lucy!"

I stopped screaming and looked to my left. There was a window in the wall, little more than a gap in the masonry. Looking and reaching through the gap was Joe.

"Joe!"

He hushed me. "Quiet, we don't want to draw their attention. Climb in through the window here."

I eyed the size of the window and realised it was a hopeless option.

"I can't," I said. "My skirt. But Leila can."

I turned to my friend and saw that she was pale. Her shirt was soaked with blood.

"Is Nate with you?"

"He was. He's just gone to the back of the church in case anyone else arrives."

Leila stepped to the window and smiled wanly.

"I'm fine. I'll stay with Lucy."

"Don't. You're injured. Just go in with Joe. I'll make my way to the door."

She looked at me, her eyes glistening. She turned away and Joe helped her in through the narrow window.

Joe leaned through the window to me.

"I'm so glad you made it," he said. "I'll go to the door. Give me a minute."

I waited a few seconds after he disappeared from sight before I followed along the wall. The entrance was stepped out from the main building by about a metre. I peered around the wall to check how many zombies were there. Four zombies remained camping out by the door. I noticed that some loose brickwork had fallen to the ground alongside the wall.

I placed my candlestick down and grabbed a couple of the rocks. I poked my head around the corner and threw one of the large rocks down the path. It drew their attention when it landed. I threw another, aiming to land it further down the path, but it landed in the garden bed, and the noise was muffled.

One of the zombies turned back to the door, and I decided it was time to act.

I said a quick prayer that Joe was in place and darted out from cover. I hit the first zombie before he noticed me, jabbing him in the stomach and knocking him to the ground.

The other zombies turned towards the falling body, and I moved to the front door, placing my back against it so I could watch the remaining zombies.

I knocked quietly and hissed out Joe's name.

The zombies kept watching their fallen comrade, and the door didn't move behind me, so I knocked again.

"Joe?"

The zombies heard me this time and turned in my direction. I was pressed against the door, surrounded by brambles that stopped me from swinging my candlestick and without enough room behind me to ram with it.

I knocked and called more frantically.

As the first zombie lurched forward, I braced the candlestick on the ground in front of me. His arms were long enough that if I did manage to hold him at bay with the candlestick, he would still be able to reach my arms.

"Joe!" I was becoming desperate.

The zombie lunged, there was a rush of air behind me, hands grasped my arms, and I was whisked backwards into darkness.

February 14, 4:25 p.m.
The bride finds a groom

The door was slammed as soon as I was through, plunging the room into semi-darkness.

"Joe?" I turned around in the arms that encased me and kissed my almost-husband.

"Are you okay?" he asked.

"Not really." I laugh-cried. "Sorry I'm late. There were a few issues with zombies, had to take a few detours."

He squeezed me tight and kissed me on the head, then gagged.

"God, that smells foul. Too much hairspray?"

I cringed. "Oooh, I wouldn't do that right now. I don't know what I'm covered with."

"Eurgh." He wiped his hand on his sleeve.

"Come this way."

He grabbed my hand and guided me over the rough ground. I tried not to let my candlestick clang on anything. Daylight shone through a doorway on the opposite wall. He led me through to a room where the roof had collapsed, opening the space to daylight and an overflow of wild roses.

"Oh, it's lovely here," I said.

"Oh my God, Lucy!" Joe said.

I turned to him and saw a look of horror on his face.

"What?"

I touched my head and looked over my body for injuries. Nothing. Only the chafing from my beaded bodice and blisters on my feet hurt.

I looked at Joe and noticed how clean he was. He had a few dirty scuffs on his suit jacket, but his black suit was otherwise unmarked, and his white shirt was...still white.

"Ah."

I looked over myself again. My dress had blood spatters and a bloody handprint, dirt caked at the knees and on the hem, grass seeds caught in the lace and several tears in the tulle.

God only knew how my hair and make-up had fared.

"What happened to you?" He asked.

"Too much to say now. How about you? You got here okay?"

"Yes, we arrived just after twelve, had our photos taken, did our checks of the marquee and settled in to wait in the chapel.

"Guests started arriving at quarter past two. A few people looked a little unwell, but there weren't any problems otherwise. Then an older lady had a seizure. When she came to, she attacked the person who had been helping her."

I groaned. I wanted to ask who, but it was too early to start counting the toll.

"We went back into the little room the minister gets ready in—"

"Vestry," I said automatically.

"—and tried to call you to see what we should do. When you didn't answer, we decided that we should move the ceremony outside.

"But your mum had arrived, and she wasn't happy with the idea at all."

Of course she wasn't. Joe described how Mother had pitched a fit. By the time they calmed her, more people had assembled in the church.

Joe and one of his groomsmen had stepped outside to check for a place to move the ceremony to, with only 25 minutes' notice, only to find that more people were turning into zombies and it was getting real.

"There were about a dozen people crammed in the vestry when I came over here about forty-five minutes ago. I came out to see if I could find you, check whether you were holed up somewhere. That's when I ran into Nate. We came across some zombies and hid in here."

"Where is Nate?"

I jumped. I had forgotten that Leila was there.

Her voice was strained, and she was holding her shoulder. Blood dribbled through her fingers

"Your shoulder! Come here. Let me look at it."

She stumbled into the room, her right arm held across her body, her face pale.

"Nate went back to the church to bring out the people who weren't zombies. There's more space here and areas we can barricade people if they turn into zombies."

"He's out there?" She asked. Her voice was shrill.

"Shhhh," I soothed. "Nate will be okay. I'm sure he had a weapon of some kind to defend himself, right?"

Joe nodded.

I guided Leila to a large pile of rubble in the middle of the space and sat her down.

"Joe, can I have your hanky?"

He pulled a hanky and a wad of tissues from his pocket.

I peeled the neck of Leila's t-shirt back and exposed a ragged oval wound. It was very clearly a bite, with two bleeding arcs surrounding an untouched patch of skin. I hissed. It looked nasty.

"How bad is it?" Leila asked.

I didn't quite know how to answer. "It looks painful."

She agreed.

"I arranged to have a big first aid kit in the vestry. We'll go and get it and bring Nate and the others back with us. In the meantime, apply pressure with this."

I bundled up Nate's hanky with the last of the tissues from my bodice and pressed them against her shoulder.

"Can you manage that?" I asked.

She nodded. There were tears in the corners of her eyes.

"I want to come with you. I need to see Nate."

I imagined all they had been through together in the last few months. Of course she needed him.

"We'll find him, I promise."

"Leila," Joe said. "There's a back way out of here, but we might have to come back in through the front because it's a quicker path and I don't want to lead them to our escape route. Can you wait by the front door and let us in when we call out?"

She nodded, tears spilling over now.

"We'll be back, I promise."

She nodded and stood, moving back to sit near the door.

Joe grabbed my hand again and led me through a few connecting rooms to a half-rotten door.

"I see why you don't want to lead the zombies here," I said.

Joe squeezed my hand before letting go and opening the door as quietly as he could. First, he opened it just wide enough to peek through, then wide enough to fit his head through, before he finally opened it fully.

"We're clear." He said.

I followed him through the door, candlestick at the ready. It was getting unwieldy and slipped from my hand, clanging on the pavers underfoot.

Joe reached out. "Let me take that."

I handed it over but felt terribly vulnerable without something to defend myself with.

I scoured the ground and spied a pile of old steel fence posts next to the stone wall. I worked one free of the pile. It was weighty but manageable.

"Here," I said and passed another fence post to him.

He thanked me and laid the candlestick down. He picked up another two fence posts and held them in his left hand.

"For the others." He said.

He led me through the empty gateway and along the path to the back of the church. We crouched and ran across the open ground to the vestry door.

Joe knocked and called out. "Hello? Is there anyone in there?"

We waited a tense moment, our breath coming heavily as we listened with our ears near the door.

The door opened slowly.

"Who is it?" came a whisper.

"Joe and Lucy, let us in."

The door was drawn wide, and we hurried through.

A banshee shriek pierced the silence before the door was fully closed behind us.

"Lucy!"

There was a blur of pastel, and mother was upon me.

"Look at the state of you, all this blood and dirt. What have you been doing? Are those sticks in your hair? And where is your veil?"

Her voice had barely dropped below the pitch of a standard dog whistle.

A hand appeared from behind her and clamped over her mouth.

Mother's face grew red with rage, and I took a step back to avoid the impending explosion.

Dad's face appeared over her shoulder.

"Dorothea." His voice was quiet but perfectly audible in the silence left after her shrieking. "This is not the time for one of your conniptions. Those *things* can hear us and will come running. For the sake of everyone in this room, be quiet."

He removed his hand from her mouth slowly.

"Conniption!" She said as soon as her mouth was free.

Dad clamped his hand back over her mouth.

"Mother," I said. "He's right. Be quiet, or I'll get them to gag you."

I had no patience left for her manipulation.

Her eye blazed at me, but she nodded her agreement. Dad pulled his hand away again. She started muttering to herself.

I ignored her.

I scanned the room. Joe was talking quietly to Nate, whose face had gone pale. Lyon was also in the room. He stepped forward and hugged me.

"I was so worried about you." He whispered in my ear.

"You too," I said.

It wasn't a complete lie. When I realised what was going on, I had been worried for my family.

Two of Joe's groomsmen were there, a few cousins and a small girl I did not recognise.

Ten people in total. Of the 250 people invited to the wedding. Not everyone had arrived, though. Maybe some people had heard the advice to stay home before it was time to leave for the ceremony and were holed up safely.

I prayed to whoever would listen that that was the case.

"Alright," I said, "someone grab me that first aid kit. Someone else grab the box of snacks and water. And everyone else grab something you can use as a weapon.

"Let's get out of here."

February 14, 4:37 p.m.
Perspective

Everybody gathered around the door with their burdens, waiting behind Nate. Nate was waiting for everyone to be signal that they were ready.

"Why?" Mother asked.

"What?" I said.

I turned to look at her. She hadn't moved since I'd threatened to gag her.

"Why do we need to leave? We're perfectly safe here. There aren't any of those things to attack us."

I groaned.

"Because there are plenty of those things on the other side of that door," Joe said, pointing to the chapel. "Any minute now, they could figure out that we're in here and bash it down."

"Not to mention that my injured wife is out there in the rectory on her own."

Mother sniffed. "Well, I'm sure she's survived worse."

I have never been so inclined to slap my mother in my life.

"Enough. We're going. Stay or come with us. It's up to you."

"But Lucy—"

"No."

I turned back to the door.

"Ready?" Nate asked.

I locked eyes with him and nodded.

He opened the door slowly, copying Joe's routine from earlier.

Finally, the door was wide open, and we trooped out. The people with weapons formed a defensive ring around the people with burdens. The little girl had been given the basket with the food and water and Dad had the first aid kit.

Mother pushed her way past me to stand next to Dad. I held my fence post away, so I wasn't tempted to whack her with it as she passed. We rounded the back of the church and followed the path between the chapel and the rectory to the front door.

As I had come to expect, a horde of zombies appeared when we reached the front of the church.

This bunch looked like a group of wedding guests with a couple of catering staff thrown in for good measure. I was pretty sure I also saw the minister.

We stopped as a group.

I assessed the situation: 10 of us, 30 of them.

They weren't great odds, and I was about to make them worse.

"Nate? Why don't you take the first aid kit, this young lady and my parents into the rectory through the back door? We'll make sure none of this lot follows you and come in through the front. We told Leila to wait by the front door. Call out to her when you go in, so you don't scare her."

Nate nodded.

"Come on then, everyone."

"I'm coming with you," Dad said to me.

"It's not safe, Dad," I said.

"I know," he said. "But it would be pretty poor of me to let my kids walk into danger without going with them."

"What about me?" Mum whined.

"Dorothea, the same offer stands as before. I'm going with the group. You make up your own mind. I won't let you sway me on this."

When we left the vestry, Joe had held on to two of his fence posts. Now, he handed one to Dad.

"Right," Nate said. "We're off."

He collected the first aid kit and guided the girl out of the group.

Mother watched him leave without her, then looked

back at the group of zombies, apparently uncertain.

Finally, she huffed at us, turned and hurried after Nate.

We turned back to the zombies.

It seemed as though they hadn't heard us so far. They were still milling about aimlessly.

"Slowly," I whispered.

We moved along the side of the church as a group, almost matching our steps with each other.

We were only 10 metres from the front of the wall when a zombie turned down the lane towards us.

Lyon swore quietly, but this zombie seemed to have good hearing. It charged towards him.

Joe stepped forward and whacked the zombie in the throat just as he was about to lunge at Lyon.

I don't know whether it was Joe's grunt of exertion, the zombie going down or Lyon's squeak of fear, but one of the noises drew the attention of the zombie horde.

We all froze as more than a dozen zombies turned their heads to look at us.

One of the zombies broke first.

A well-built older gentleman in a suit barrelled towards Joe, followed by a woman in black—who wears black to a wedding—who moved towards Lyon.

Before I could track what was happening with them, I noticed that Dad was under attack.

He raised his steel fence post just as Aunt Beryl attacked. I saw in snapshots. She lunged. He jabbed. She fell onto the fence post. He fell backwards, the other end of the fence post aiming for his heart. He rolled to the left and threw his arms to the right. His face blanched with pain as Aunt Beryl fell on him.

"Dad!"

I rushed to his side.

He was breathing heavily, and blood seeped from his side.

I knelt down on the ground beside him, touching his chest.

"Hu...hu..." he said.

"I know, Dad. I know. Where does it hurt?"

All the dramas of the wedding, dress and zombie fight forgotten, I found Dad's hand and squeezed. I was prepared to stay with him as he died, even if it meant waiting for another zombie to fall on me.

Aunt Beryl had gone limp when she fell on him, the fence post doing enough damage to kill her properly.

"Hu...Her...heavy."

I bobbed back on my heels, confused.

"She's...heavy...get...off."

"Oh!" I said.

I pushed at Aunt Beryl's shoulder and hip, levering her off Dad.

He groaned as the weight moved.

"I...always knew she'd...try to kill me."

"Are you okay?" I asked.

He sat, and I saw that he'd thrown the fence post away from his body as he rolled. He'd only been winded from the impact of Aunt Beryl's substantial frame. The blood on his side was hers.

His gaze was caught by something over my right shoulder, and his eyes widened.

"Duck."

Instinctively, I did exactly as he said. I ducked down and to the left, away from the zombie I assumed had caught his attention.

There was a whoosh over my head, a thwack and then a fine mist sprayed over us before the body thudded to the ground.

"Get up!"

Someone gave the instruction and offered a hand to me.

I let him haul me to my feet and then turned to make sure Dad was up.

"Over here!"

I followed the sound of Joe's voice. He was standing next to the rectory where the low garden wall met the wall of the house. About 8 metres from the corner.

"We can avoid them by going over the wall."

I pushed Dad along and reached down for my fence post.

"Lucy, hurry!" Joe urged.

Dad had made it to the wall and was being helped over, leaving only Joe, Greg and me on this side of the garden wall.

I reached the wall, looked at the uneven rocks and the height and realised it was impossible.

I would have had no trouble if I'd been in shorts or even jeans. But I had no chance in the monstrosity of a dress.

"I can't," I said. "I'll go the long way."

"Of course you can," Joe said. "There isn't any other way now."

I glanced towards the marquee and cemetery and saw that he was right. There was no way out down there now. The lane was clogged with bodies. A glance towards the back of the buildings showed that our commotion had also drawn zombies from that direction. From the car park, I assumed.

"Shit."

"See. You have to go over."

"It's not that I don't want to. It's this damn dress. Hold this."

Giving in, I gave Joe my fence post and assessed my options.

The rock wall was about 90 centimetres high. It should have been easy to get over but not in this dress. I would need to hold my skirts, but then I wouldn't be able to boost myself with my hands.

I turned back to face Joe. "I can't do it."

"We don't have time!"

Joe grabbed me by the waist, shuffled me two steps to my right, lifted me off the ground by a tiny amount and tipped me over the fence backwards.

My head, torso and butt fell over the fence and landed in lush, squishy foliage that softened my fall.

"Roll." He shouted.

Automatically, I pulled my legs up to my body, scraping my calves on the rough rock. I rolled to my left and only then did I realise that he'd thrown me into a patch of rose briars.

While the lush growth had stopped me from hitting the pavers, I wasn't happy about the scratches from the thorns. Then again, worse things had happened today. I would cope.

The scratches on my shoulders and arms stung, though.

Joe was over the fence and lifting me to my feet. He dragged me backwards to the cottage door because he'd taken off before I found my feet under the hoop skirt or had turned around.

Noticing Joe's difficulty, Greg grabbed me under my right arm. Joe adjusted his grip on my left arm, and they dragged me backwards to safety.

I would be amazed if there were any beads left on the back of my dress after this.

We reached the door of the old cottage, and it was thrown wide to allow us entry.

Although we hadn't been followed over the fence by any zombies, we hurried inside. Someone slammed the door shut behind us, plunging the room into darkness.

The room was filled with the sounds of heavy breathing as we collectively gathered our breath and lowered our heart rates.

The silence was pierced by a shriek that was cut off as quickly as it began.

My heart rate kicked back up again, and I hurried to the doorway leading to the section of the house that was open to the sky.

I found Mother standing in the middle of the courtyard, Nate's hand clamped over her mouth as she looked at Dad with wide, horror-filled eyes.

Of course, he was covered in blood. She was worried about him.

"No more screaming," Nate said. "Do you understand?"

Mother nodded, and Nate removed her hand.

"Oh Clinton! What happened? You have completely ruined that shirt..."

I tuned out the rest of her tirade. Seriously, that woman needed some perspective. And it looked like there was someone about to give it to her.

"Enough," Leila said. "Honestly, Dorothea, I have tried to be polite to you, but I am out of patience today. Have you not seen what is happening?"

"Yes, Lucy's wedding is ruined—"

"The *world* is ruined, you stupid woman. The wedding is the least of it. There are so many things going on in the world that are bigger than you and your petty regret that you got knocked up before you were married. I'm sick of hearing about it, and I'm sick of you making Lucy feel guilty about it. No more."

Mum was shocked into silence. Thankfully.

"Now," Leila said. "We've finally got you two together and we have someone who is permitted to perform weddings in the room. Shall we get you married?"

February 14, 5:00 p.m.
Mr and Mrs

"I am a person duly authorised by law to solemnise marriages and officiate at your marriage today," Nate said.

Our dozen wedding guests had gathered in the room in the middle of the old rectory that was open to the sky and filled with roses.

Leila's shoulder wound had been cleaned and bandaged. We snipped away the bloodiest portions of her shirt and held it together with safety pins.

The make-up remover wipes in the first aid kit had been put to good use to wipe my scratches from the rose bush. Joe had wrapped bandages around my upper arms to cover my scrapes, and I'd dug out some bandaids for my blisters.

Mother was sulking in a corner.

She'd come to me to complain about how Leila spoke to her. She wasn't very happy when I told her that I didn't want to hear her complain and I wasn't going to let her tell me what to do. I also threatened to throw her out with the zombies if she whined, complained or insulted anyone.

The little girl collected a bouquet of small roses from the runners invading the room for me. I tied them together with a piece of tulle torn from the hem of my dress. There were way too many layers of the stuff anyway.

Joe wore blood spatters, and I wore bloody handprints, splashes of gore and a dead woman's boots. And we were both ridiculously happy to have made it to our altar of broken roof tiles.

The ceremony was simple, neither of us remembered our vows and neither of us cared. We were just glad that the groomsman with the rings had made it to the altar with us.

It was messy and small and officiated by our friend.

Although we were rocky at that moment, I had my best friend by my side, and I knew we would build up our friendship again.

The world was a mess. Although it would be fleeting, we grabbed our moment of happiness and squeezed everything we could out of it.

And despite all that had happened, it seemed Mother's wish had been granted.

It was a wedding we'd be telling our grandchildren about.